A Friday in August

D0274398

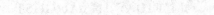

ANTONIO D'ALFONSO

A FRIDAY IN AUGUST

A Novel

TRANSLATED FROM THE FRENCH BY JO-ANNE ELDER

TORONTO

Exile Editions

2005

Originally published as *Un vendredi du mois d'août*,
Leméac éditeur Inc., 2004
Copyright © Antonio D'Alfonso and Leméac éditeur Inc., 2004.
Translation © Jo-Anne Elder and Exile Editions, 2005.
All rights reserved. The use of any part of this publication, reproduced,
transmitted in any form or by any means, electronic, mechanical,
photocopying, recording or otherwise stored in a retreieval system,
without the prior consent of the publisher is an infringement of the
copyright law.

This edition is published by Exile Editions Limited, 20 Dale Ave.,
Toronto, Ontario, Canada M4W 1KA
Telephone: 416 485 9468
www.ExileEditions.com

Sales Distribution:
McArthur & Company c/o Harper Collins
1995 Markham Road, Toronto, ON M1B 5M8
toll free: 1 800 387 0117 (fax) 1 800 668 5788

Library and Archives Canada Cataloguing in Publication
D'Alfonso, Antonio
[Vendredi du mois d'août. English]
A Friday in August / Antonio D'Alfonso ;
translated by Joe-Anne Elder.
Translation of: Un vendredi du mois d'août.
ISBN 1-55096-639-1
I. Elder, Joe-Anne II. Title.
III. Title: Vendredi du mois d'août. English.
PS8557.A456V4613 2005 C843'.54 C2005-906700-4
Design and Composition: ADA
Cover Lithograph: Claire Weissman Wilks
Printed in Canada: Gauvin Imprimerie

The author wishes to thank Jo-Anne Elder, Barry Callaghan,
and Elana Wolff for their reading and editorial suggestions.
Financial support for this translation provided by the Canada Council
for the Arts and the Department of Canadian Heritage through the
Book Publishing Industry Development Program.
The publisher wishes to acknowledge the assistance toward publication
of the Canada Council for the Arts.

Canada Council   Conseil des Arts
for the Arts   du Canada

Nous sommes des créatures tellement mobiles, que les senti-
ments que nous feignons, nous finissons par les épreuver.
Benjamin Constant,
Adolphe (1816)

[We are such changeable creatures that we eventually
come to experience the feelings that we counterfeit.
Translated by Margaret Mauldon]

I

"Where's the cream for my coffee? It was here yesterday morning. Who's stolen my cream?"

I nearly die laughing.

I haven't eaten any dairy products for nearly ten years.

This is today's fight. Yesterday, it was something else that made Ada mad at me.

It's a delayed reaction. They all are. She'll use any excuse to jump down my throat. This time it's the cream. Another time it was because I left my shoes in the living room.

She's highly volatile. Unpredictable. Ada explodes. All of a sudden, some slight from months back will pass through her tiny body and the little bumpy road of our relationship becomes a roller-coaster ride. When Ada lets loose, everything comes out. In an instant, the mood changes and a day-long rage will begin.

I have trouble believing that so much fury can be contained for months at a time in her body.

I, on the other hand, react right away when something bothers me. I flare up, on the spot, usually before the situation has a chance to deteriorate into an incident.

These days, I burst out laughing when Ada shows her first signs of rage. This makes her anger four times worse.

We go after each other, without drawing knives, of course, and often we can't even remember what started the latest fight.

Ada locks everything away inside of herself, chewing away at her sad condition and her worries thirty-three times, the way you're supposed to chew your vegetables, before swallowing them. Is it a sign of some survival instinct? Self-protection?

No doubt she suffered a lot as a teenager.

Not really knowing who was to blame, what happened, I imagine her pain has its source in some distant sorrow.

I'm not a doctor, though, and it isn't my job to peel away the shell in which the woman I love is living. I make it a practice to never mix love and psychoanalysis.

The important thing is to live together with some sort of dignity.

Sharing our common and busy lives together is what builds love. Not the baggage we carry around with us, or these little dialogues prescribed by the experts who claim they're supposed to be healthy for a couple.

I know that the kind of thing that is confessed in a therapist's office can be repeated, later on, at a party with friends.

The mistake is in thinking that love is all it takes to satisfy your sweetheart's every need. Sleeping in the same bed, making love, studying, eating, taking a walk with the person you love, separating and getting back together – these are all very complex activities in the life of a couple.

The other person is there to appreciate and be appreciated. Not to analyze or be analyzed.

Which is why I find it necessary to laugh.

Laughter doesn't solve every problem. It helps. That's all.

If I need to get my pipes cleaned out, I call a plumber.

When Ada had her appendicitis, she didn't ask me to perform an appendectomy. We rushed off to the hospital. This was not the time to play doctor.

I think that the blues musician Willie Dixon must have figured something out about couples when he sang, "I just want to make love to you."

You have to be able to love your life's partner for what she or he is. Imagine signing a contract with someone based on what he is supposed to be.

What right do I have to ask the woman I love to change?

Some people I know tell me that Ada reacts so dramatically because she's jealous. What should she be jealous about? Or who? That's what I'd like to know.

I work so hard that sometimes I fall asleep before I'm even finished masturbating.

I don't try to figure out the reasons for her behaviour, her temper tantrums. She has no reason to be jealous. I've never played around.

I try to laugh to show her my affection and my respect for her. I'm afraid it doesn't always work.

2

A long road winds upward in a spiral to a blue stucco house.

Ada is wearing a red cotton dress over her magnificent olive-toned skin.

She walks towards the house.

It's summer. A narrow doorway separates day and night.

Her irrepressible curiosity propels Ada towards her destination. She is ignoring the warnings I'm shouting at her.

She bounds towards this door of clouds. She places her hand on the translucent doorknob and summer is transformed into a sea of stars.

Ada says, "We're floating in the bloodstream of a powerful land."

I don't understand what she's saying, and I ask her to explain.

She says, "It's normal for you not to understand. No one understands all this stuff about paradise. Not in the slightest. Despite our scientific developments and our advanced technology, we're still too little and our view's too narrow to see the world in all its wholeness. You have to be satisfied with rushing like a busy ant over the sands of time and space. Don't you see? The night is thick and the furniture is covered in dust."

I say, "I can see a lightning bolt on the horizon, above your shoulders."

She says, "Are you afraid?"

I nod my head. "Yes, I'm scared, deep down inside me.

But I don't know what I'm afraid of, because nothing frightens me and I frighten no one."

She laughs. "One day you'll see how things around you fit together, and you'll finally understand. Right now, just follow me."

Ada takes my hand, holds it tight, I know she can feel the fear that vibrates through me, the sky melts into the sea, and everywhere there is water transformed into bicycle wheels, and we are there, side by side, pedalling our way down a gravel path that leads us to the family home, in Molise, Italy.

The wind is gentle, we laugh with pleasure, I push my fingers over Ada's thighs, there's no one around. Why are these pebbles so utterly unfamiliar?

Ada says, "Stand your bicycle up against the wall and follow me."

I say, "I am having a really weird dream."

I describe the magical, celestial sea that has brought us to this countryside landscape.

Ada bursts out laughing. "It's not a dream, you cucumber, we're really here. Can't you see the ashes from the stars all over your shoulders?"

I love it when she calls me "cucumber." Cucumbers are my favourite vegetable. I devour them.

I examine my shirt which, indeed, is covered in grey soot.

Ada walks into the house where my father grew up, and suddenly I have my back up against the wall of military latrines in the downtown core of a large city where soldiers with scalded skin and charred faces piss all over me.

Neither wish nor fantasy, what starts off as a pleasant dream, almost erotic, ends up as a nightmare.

A cheap book on dreams would tell you that urine is a metaphor for poor health, revealing the way illness is likely to affect the behaviour of the analysand towards his friends.

Dreaming that people are pissing on me would, therefore, signify that my friendships and love affairs are pretty much going down the drain right now.

In other words, I'm down on my luck.

3

Far from sublimating my fantasies, I am prey to an unconscious that signals misfortune.

Failure is the inability to master what you believe you have mastered. You've been dealt a bad hand. The hardest thing is to admit you've failed.

For a long time, I believed I was an artist. I even made a couple of films that critics and audiences adored. I love what I do, even if my films aren't always that great. I can convince myself that I've finished a piece, but the truth is I never finish anything. I am a hard-working man held captive by laziness.

I have to clarify everything, say the things that ought not be said. I go after the whole world, complaining that people in power are cruel and unjust. Inevitably, I have to sit down and admit that I'm the one who's guilty of making all these mistakes. No one else is to blame.

Maybe it's true. Maybe I'm a mediocre artist.

When did this insecurity first rear its ugly head? I have no idea. I don't remember anything.

I was always unpopular. Everybody always told me I was a good-for-nothing. So I finally threw it all away.

TV, fridge, clock, plasticized shoes, everything. What would I do with my naked body? Nothing much, except maybe feel guilty for all the living things I killed to feed myself. I'm an emotional cannibal.

Even though, for the past ten years, I haven't eaten meat. I don't want to eat anything with a face, as Paul McCartney puts it.

When certain people open their mouths, I can see that their teeth have torn apart the flesh of a pig or a cow. The strips of skin stay stuck on their gums, like a lie that stays pressed against someone's eyeballs. Sometimes I detect the odour of animal blood on their tongue.

I get a big kick out of weeping when I watch a sappy film on TV.

4

Ada and Rasa are sleeping in their respective rooms. Ada and I don't share a bed. It has been like that since the beginning. When Ada asked me if it would bother me to go sleep in the living room, I didn't hold it against her. I understand her need to have a room all to herself.

Anyway, Ada and I don't have the same dentist, don't go to the same optometrist, and don't vote for the same political party.

I only need four hours of sleep; Ada needs at least eight. She is a doctor in family practice, and her days are horribly long.

I don't say anything, but secretly I envy couples who, at night, can feel the warmth of another pair of feet under the covers.

My eyes prickle. I look out the window of the dormer window and can see my Portuguese neighbour playing with her children. The heat wave persists.

Fatima is trying to put buttered toast into the mouths of her sons, those two thundering bucks, built like workhorses and bright-eyed like Pan. Her husband, wearing a dark suit, drinks his espresso and gets ready to go to work. He's a shoe salesman.

His sister-in-law, Kathy, who just separated from her husband, has rented two rooms. She lives there with Maddy, her budding intellectual, whose head is invariably bent over a novel, and Gianni, her six-year-old son, who is practising for the next World Cup.

In the air an aroma of breakfast wafts over from my other neighbours, the widow, Lorie, and her son, Angelo, a sound engineer for the public radio network.

I walk down to the kitchen, where yesterday's pasta plastered to the plates looks like cardboard puzzle pieces. I was too tired to clear the table. No plot can keep the inevitable from playing out. I was so moved by an American B movie that I forgot to wash the dishes before I went to bed.

I throw out the leftovers in a bag of compost. I clean everything up before Ada wakes up. She doesn't like being faced with garbage when she wakes up.

I drink a glass of grapefruit juice while I read the *Globe and Mail*, *La Repubblica*, and *Il Corriere Canadese* which I've gathered from the doorstep. I haven't had a cup of coffee for years. I'm nervous enough as it is. If I manage to get through the pages of the right-wing daily that the *Globe and Mail* is, it's only because of *La Repubblica*, which comes to me directly from Italy.

"You can't claim to be an intellectual if you don't know what the right wing is thinking," Barry Callaghan tells me. He's one of the greatest writers in English Canada. You have to know what your enemy is thinking in order to understand your own thoughts.

Barry's right. You have to know everything in order to be able to grasp hold of the little details of current events.

I go back up into the attic and pull on a pair of pants, a T-shirt, red socks and sneakers. I gallop out of the house.

Is it the heat of the morning, or my white pants that are sticking to my skin?

I'm not dressed for any serious hiking.

Still, here I am, bent over after a few minutes, out of breath, with a heartbeat racing so fast it makes me think my chest is going to explode. I clutch my ribs and breathe quickly, swallowing the disgusting downtown air in great mouthfuls. I will never live far enough away from the city's grime and racket.

In this morning's *Corriere*, they're talking about the black medal that Toronto has won, as the most polluted city in Canada. More than 88,498 tonnes of toxic chemicals are flushed into Ontario's atmosphere every year. It's not surprising that Rasa suffers from asthma.

5

My breathing is terrible. Asthma is a weak excuse for the lazy man I've become. To tell the truth, I'm not at all asthmatic. I have to invent some reason for not working this morning, the 31st of August.

Ordinarily, I motor on day and night. My fervent dedication is something Ada admires but could live without. I work too much. Today, buried in my chair, I will stagnate in front of my computer screens, daydreaming.

I don't remember who it was who said that a workaholic is, deep down, a lazy man. Whoever it was, he was right.

When I lived in Montreal, I ran for an hour around the Parc Lafontaine, without ever needing to stop to get my breath.

Since I've been living in the capital of Ontario, I've dropped my physical fitness routine and my yoga. At best, I recite the mantra my yogi gave me, like a secret, without taking myself too seriously, when I need to relax. That's about it. In general, smoking a cigarette at the right moment will do it.

One will never reach nirvana by cheating. And anyway, I don't want to go to the paradise of the dead before my time comes.

I laugh as I think of the joke a film editor told me yesterday. Two friends have been in heaven for two thousand years.

They start getting tired of listening to the same music coming from the celestial harps all the time. They decide to talk to St. Peter, to find out if there's any other place where they can go to have fun.

St. Peter says, "Yes, there is a place. You simply have to walk down the stairs and turn left."

The two friends look at each other and say that they'd really like to go there. The saint gives them permission for a short outing.

The buddies make their way down and turn left at the bottom of the staircase, where they stop in front of a huge gate. They knock. Someone comes to open the gate. They can hear dance music.

They go in and find themselves among magnificent, naked women who greet them with open arms. It's sheer bliss. They make love all night long and into the morning. But it's already time to come back to heaven.

St. Peter opens the door and lets them in. A thousand years go by.

The friends go back to see the saint who gives them another leave, so that they can go back to see their conquests downstairs. After another weekend of mad love, the friends return to heaven.

A thousand years go by.

Again, they meet St. Peter who, this time, seems less inclined to satisfy their wishes. The saint says, "Listen, you have to choose. Stay there or stay here."

The friends look at each other and make their final decision.

"We'd like to live on the lower level."

St. Peter asks them, "Are you sure?"

The buddies say, "Yes."

St. Peter opens the gate and, as soon as the two men have gone downstairs, he locks the gate.

The friends, ecstatic, never turn back to look at the paradise they've lost.

When they get to the gate at the bottom of the stairs, they knock, giddy with joy.

Strangely, there is no answer.

They knock again.

Nothing.

They knock a third time, and suddenly someone unlocks the gate.

Lucifer grabs them by the collar and pushes them violently against the wall where a dozen men stab them with burning forks.

The friends cry out, "Stop! What's going on here? This isn't the first time we've been here, you know."

Lucifer bursts out laughing. "Before, you were tourists. Now you're immigrants. Welcome to Hell!"

6

I haven't exactly made the kind of films that bring tears to my dreamy-eyed viewers. Except for a few documentaries on drugs and organized crime, my illusions are rather modest inventions.

I once filmed a hit-man who had more to say than the novelists I met in Toronto. His life was full of dead bodies. Before he killed them, he held intense discussions on the meaning of life that left them perplexed. According to him, what mattered most was honesty: a guy could commit the worst crimes imaginable, but if and when he was caught, he shouldn't demean or belittle what he had done.

This criminal didn't take himself for some kind of god. He wasn't just following the orders of some capo. He could always predict who needed to die like a dog and who would die with dignity. Despite his sleazy job, there was nothing worthless about him.

I know genius when I see it. I can tell glitter from the gold. At my age, I've no secrets, and I don't have to invent great feats for myself anymore. Reality is my working uniform. I put it on every morning and I don't complain about it. I'm almost glad. Happiness has finally settled into my life, and I am proud of it.

What counts isn't glory or brilliant success. It's the process. All I need is an honest smile at the end of the day, and then I can take my refuge and find my place in front of the TV, where I iron my shirts, and watch a made-for-TV movie that I had refused to make.

Yesterday I tried to sell a film project to reps from a couple of big American companies. The results weren't spectacular. The producers laughed, but I couldn't tell what they really thought of the synopsis. They paid me compliments for the images I'd shot. Would they put their money where their mouth is?

I should get used to the little production studio where I've been working for twenty years. We sell fewer products than the big production houses. What matters, essentially, is working: as long as I do my work well, someone is bound to find some money for me. Despite a few bad reviews, I think our work is quite acceptable.

7

I keep telling myself I should write down all my thoughts in a journal. But I'm a bit wary of the idea. Especially since I've had the opportunity of watching my wife pitch my notebook in my face in the middle of an argument. She threw a fit about fantasies that I had never acted on. Diaries seem truer than reality. And now, one reality is plenty for me.

Why interpret a story as it is going on? I bear witness to the present by filming it. I film the present, and then I screen this present, transformed into the past. I never comment on the images.

I want to forget everything. I'm restless. My feet shake like James Brown's.

I want to sleep, relax, but I can't.

Last night, when I got home, Rasa, who has chicken pox, wanted to entertain herself by watching the movie in which Charlie Chaplin eats his shoe: *The Gold Rush*. She's been fascinated by this film since she was tiny. She especially loves the scene in which Big Jim, who is starving, imagines Charlie as a plump and juicy chicken. A great vegetarian image. Chaplin was a vegetarian.

Rasa laughed out loud, sitting there between my legs, while we ate our plates of fusilli with rapini.

Rasa cuddling up with me. This is something new for her, this desire to stay at my side. I know that she feels my fatherly protection when she's close to me, but I get the feeling it's more than that. I don't know what to call it.

Gratitude. She's discovering that Papa is more than her Mama's shadow.

These days, she speaks to me in English, in Italian, in Portuguese – her babysitter, Fatima, is Portuguese – and in French – she goes to a French school. It's moving to see her bring home sentences she has learned at school. A child is a sponge. We have to give children everything we can.

Rasa giggles when I beg her to translate Portuguese phrases into Italian. What a pleasure it gives me to watch this little five-year-old girl dance among the languages. A lovely ballet.

One night, she was searching for the French word for *bark*. The word *écorce* slipped my mind. I had to look it up in the dictionary. Rasa burst out laughing. "Papa! You don't know French!"

Indeed, she has a point: with all the languages I have spinning around in my head, I don't know which one to speak.

8

I always have fun at the movies. I usually laugh in the wrong places. Friends have pointed this out to me more than once.

I crack up before they get to the joke.

My hilarity, wherever it occurs, rings out in guffaws of gratitude for the filmmaker who has managed to lift my spirits by telling me the story of his life. A simple anecdote is the exclamation of his whole being; he is sharing with me all the love he has stored up inside him. It is as though it's dedicated to me.

Laughter is the expression of my amazement. I laugh instead of clapping. I laugh the way people underline a passage in a book when it resonates deep inside their hearts.

I cry the way I laugh. Tears are often a variant of laughter. Don't we sometimes have tears in our eyes from laughing hard at a particularly good joke? We cry when laughter is no longer enough to help us take in the wholeness, the intensity, of the moment. We burst into tears or laughter; we laugh tears of joy.

We laugh once the life-threatening illness has been cured. We laugh until we have tears in our eyes.

But laughter is the gesture that children take the most time to understand, and to imitate. Rasa cried the second she came into the world. Imagine Rasa coming out of her mother's tummy and bursting into laughter! What a beautiful sight!

For months I haven't had any urge to laugh. I'm contented, but I don't laugh the way I used to. How can you cry or laugh in the face of a child's suffering? Rasa has chicken pox. A child is the gift of the earth. She can take control of your entire existence. I'm worried: I can't let her scratch, or she might be marked for life.

Gianni Moretti, in *Caro Diario*, shows how children can easily transform the situation into terror when the relationship of a couple is out of whack. Moretti is a filmmaker of my generation, the only Italian artist whose work speaks to me today.

I realize that I reveal secrets that shouldn't be spoken in public. I tell myself that I don't have any secrets.

I speak such nonsense that everyone can figure out, sooner or later, what I'm thinking and feeling and eating at any given time. I'm unable to keep my life to myself. I listen a lot, but sometimes not very well. I'm relentlessly present, always fully with the people I'm with. Meeting people is the glorious manifestation of one's presence in the world. Without presence, all is lost. Paradoxically, I tape what escapes me. If vanity is the driving force of the world, it doesn't mean much when it comes to talking about presence.

The smell of rice, garlic, potatoes, onions, and tomatoes pulls me out of my reverie. These are the gentle fragrances of tomorrow's supper. Of course, I love pasta. There's also the incantation of riso aborio. A risotto with mushrooms is just as wonderful as penne arrabiata. Let's not waste time. Let's get to work.

9

Ada. I met her the first night I arrived in Toronto.

Jennifer, a friend, a relatively well-known English-Canadian actress, introduced us.

I was out having a drink with a colleague when I caught sight of Jennifer crossing Queen Street.

I invited her to have a martini with us.

She had barely finished her drink when she invited me to have dinner at her place, in return for the favour.

Jennifer hid one little detail: she had also invited a childhood friend of hers.

Ada wore her hair short, just as I like it, and was sitting on the floor playing chess with Jennifer's daughter. Ada was wearing a pair of overalls that made her look like a Chinese labourer. It was a style that I didn't mind one bit.

I watched her in silence, as she was being beaten by her teenage opponent, and it was at that very moment that she looked like a woman who could knock me off my feet.

As soon as we had finished the meal – couscous with curry and vegetables – Ada and I found ourselves alone together in the street.

It was about three in the morning.

Ada had driven her car there. Offering her a ride home would have been absurd.

In case she wanted to talk some time, I politely slipped her a paper on which I had written the phone number of the people with whom I was shacking up in a room free of charge. An innocent gesture and, I thought, so unlikely to be seen as macho that she would have no reason to say no.

The funniest thing about it – maybe "funny" isn't exactly the right word to describe the feelings that overtook me at the time – was that she absolutely refused to even take the paper from me. She told me it wouldn't be necessary.

With my hand outstretched like a beggar, I let her know that, in any case, it had been an honour to meet her.

What else could I do, besides saying "good night" to her?

The next day, the phone rang at six in the morning.

Ada apologized for having mistreated me the night before.

I forgave her, and reassured her that her gesture had not seemed rude to me; I realized the invitation might have seemed too forward, aggressive.

She invited me out for a drink.

"At six in the morning?" I asked.

"You cucumber! After work! Let's say . . . six o'clock this evening?"

At the time, we were in the middle of filming *Antigone Pacifica*, and I absolutely had to get back to Montreal to shoot the last few scenes.

"I have to leave before seven, or I'll probably fall asleep at the wheel. It's a long trip, and I don't like driving at night."

"Let's take a rain cheque then."

I couldn't turn her down. "No, no, an hour will be plenty of time. It'll give us a chance to see if it's worth seeing each other again."

We did, indeed, meet that night, in a bar on College Street. A few months later we were living together.

IO

Here I am, more of a realist than a romantic, more interested in the environment than sports, more of a husband than a seducer. I have to concentrate, and unwrap everyone's presents before I start breathing again.

I don't feel like eating. It's not hunger that keeps me from working, but the absence of memories.

Memory comes to the surface like images boiling over, and then, more gently, flowing down my body.

The houses in our neighbourhood encourage me to continue my walk. They're built like others in North American cities, and the neighbours are reassuring. I find the pointed roofs of their Victorian design calming to my mind which, normally, resists this kind of monotony.

Even though these bland buildings don't match my glee, I'm in familiar territory. I was about to murmur "I feel at home here." But that's a concept I have trouble articulating. I'm "at home" wherever I feel good, everywhere and nowhere at the same time.

And, at this precise instant, I feel good in my running shoes, my red socks, my white pants, and my T-shirt. It's just as good as if I were wearing a tux and bow-tie.

I feel good in front of the river, or the main street that crosses the city; in front of the sea, that enormous park for worn-out big kids; in front of the ocean with its beaches of soft sands; before my editing table, the only respectable jury that has anything to say about which scenes I'll keep and which I'll throw away.

It has been impossibly hot since the first day of the month. Because of the smog, the earth is like a red kettle.

Nonetheless, I like the sticky sweat that tickles me all the way down my backside on this morning where nature plays jokes with her long, lover's fingers.

It's fine to sing praises to the beauty of snow and winter but, in my opinion, there's only one season: summer, with its cherry-tears which, suddenly, cleanse the iris of the sky. There's only one way to live, and that is by surrendering to the essential heat.

Other seasons are only sequels for a sad world that refuses to dance.

Walking around naked in my bedroom, transformed into an office – that's my real pleasure.

Contrary to many other self-employed people, I appreciate being able to work without the presence of people, solitary, at home, having a glass of barely-chilled Evian water, and lamenting, like a naughty boy, the stifling pressure of summer.

The water that slurps around my mouth reminds me that drinking behind a window covered with snow would be silly. You have to have experienced the drought of Mexico, for example, in order to better enjoy the mysteries of water on this hot summer day.

These thoughts of water make me thirsty, and I decide to go to an all-night variety store owned by a nice Korean couple.

They're the same age as I am and spend most of their time inside this little corner store. Immigrants from California, they left because it had become too violent there. They settled in Montreal for ten years before setting up shop here, a few steps away from the Korean district.

They're proud of their only child, a son, to whom they teach mathematics and Korean grammar, between sales of cigarettes or milk. Variety stores don't sell much of a variety of things, the Korean man says, making a joke of the French word *dépanneur*, which means to help out someone in a bind. They're mainly for milk-drinkers and smokers bound to their habits.

"With my bottle of grapefruit juice, what do I look like?" I ask them, in French. *"J'ai l'air de quoi?"* I laugh. *"Donnez-moi aussi un paquet de Gauloises blondes."*

We always speak to each other in French, because they don't want to forget the French they learned in Quebec.

"You're not like our other clients," jokes his wife, whose name I've never known.

The husband laughs, too, and then we all laugh together. I tell them the joke about two friends who get sick of paradise.

Before I have a chance to finish, two men with ski-masks and guns burst into the store.

One of them pushes me, the bottle crashes to the floor, and juice sprays up my pants.

The second man runs over to the cash register and puts his gun up to the wife's forehead. He takes a garbage bag out of his jacket, and shouts, "Put all the money from the cash register and all the cigarettes in this bag."

Nobody dares move. I'm down on my knees, a gun pressed to my temple. I stare at the hole from which the bullet that will end my days will be released and wipe off the annoying drop of sweat trickling down my forehead. I admire how calm the Koreans are. They know the drill.

I contain my nervousness and breathe deeply, quite deeply, the way I do when I'm repeating my mantra. Well, I think, my transcendental meditation is going to be useful for something. I open my eyes and stare into those of the man in front of the counter, who pivots around to look at his colleague, still holding his gun to my head.

The man beside me, nervous, shouts, "Hurry up!"

The other man, excited, says he's doing what he can.

I recognize the voice.

The man with the gun to my temple twists around in my direction, and his blue eyes meet mine.

Suddenly, the irony of the situation hits me like a blow.

It is Peter Hébert, my brother-in-law.

He recognizes me, too. He swears, screaming a threat in his friend's direction, complaining about how slowly the Korean woman is moving. She is phlegmatically tossing into the garbage bag every object within her reach.

She hands over the bag, filled with change and bills, cigarettes and cigars, to Peter's friend, who cries out, "Quick! Let's get out of here!"

The bandits flee.

The Korean man, visibly relieved, runs over to me.

I get up, shaken and soaked in grapefruit juice. I apologize for the mess. I shrug my shoulders helplessly and hide the fact that it was my brother-in-law who just held them up.

"There's no point getting upset. In this kind of situation, we have to realize our lives are worth a lot more than the money we've lost. They've taken maybe two hundred dollars in cash and a few hundred in cigarettes."

The husband comes back over to me with another bottle of juice.

"Here you are. Go home and rest. Don't worry. We're going to call the police."

I say good-bye.

I'm completely wet – covered in juice and sweat. I'm scared to death.

I rush back home, into the kitchen where Ada is drinking her coffee, sitting in a puffy upholstered chair in front of the window. Her morning ritual. She devours me with her eyes.

"I was involved in an armed robbery at the Koreans' just now! One of the guys was Peter."

"Peter?"

"My sister's husband."

"Peter Hébert? Are you sure?"

"He had a gun to my forehead. I'm not about to forget the look in those blue eyes of his."

"Peter isn't the only man in the world with blue eyes."

"It was definitely Peter Hébert."

Ada spits out Peter's name several times before asking me if I'm going to call Lucia.

"You have to tell your sister," she insists. "It would be stupid of you not to tell her what you've been through. What's he doing in Toronto?"

"Doesn't he have a brother here?" I ask.

She ignores me. Her eyes are on the stove clock.

"Hurry up, or you'll miss your plane."

It is almost 7:30. My flight is at 8:45.

I go down to the basement. Rasa is sitting on the toilet bowl.

"Papa, wipe me. Are you sweating?"

"I've been jogging."

Rasa stretches her whole body over my knee, tilting her bum in my direction so that I can wipe her, gently, with toilet paper. She then insists on being washed with a wet towel afterwards.

Ever since she was very small, I've told her how much healthier it is to wash with water than to wipe with paper.

Rasa pulls up her clothes and runs towards the kitchen, singing out: "Papa's sweaty, Papa's sweaty."

Rasa makes up a little song with words that rhyme with "sweaty."

I shave and jump into the shower. Under the cold blasts of water that penetrate my skin, I think of Lucia, think about how I'm going to tell her about what's happened.

Ada and Rasa drive me to the airport.

I tell Ada about an incident that took place about twenty years ago in Montreal.

I was living on my own. It was my first apartment, in the 1970s.

One night Peter rings the doorbell. He's carrying a heavy sports bag that almost drags on the ground.

"I have a favour to ask you."

He's my brother-in-law. Family. I could hardly refuse. I agree to keep his bag in the closet of the room he once helped me paint.

A week goes by, and then another.

My friend Thomas comes to see me. We're talking about painting and film.

He gets worried. Have I ever even looked in the bag to see what's in it? I say no. Thomas calls me an idiot and goes into the bedroom. He opens the door of the closet and pulls out the bag. He unzips it.

"Just as I thought!"

Packed in plastic baggies, bricks of hashish, each one, clearly stamped with its number.

"You call him immediately and order him to come and get this shit before it's too late."

Peter comes that evening to pick up his bag.

We say *ciao* quickly and he takes off with his secret into the night.

"I could never tell my sister this story," I say.

Rasa, who hasn't understood any of this, insists on having me explain what hashish is.

"A kind of chocolate," I say.

12

I get out of the car first, with my bag that's much too heavy to carry comfortably.

I kiss Ada good bye and tell her, "I love you." She says, "Break a leg."

I lean into the car and kiss Rasa on the cheek. When the time comes to leave, I pretend that my lips are stuck to her cheek. Rasa says, "Papa, don't be so childish!" I whisper to her in Italian: *"Ti amo."*

I run over to the Air Canada desk.

"Monsieur Notte? Your flight is leaving."

I thank the hostess and run towards the gate.

A second hostess, a stewardess, punches the keyboard of her computer.

"Hurry, they're waiting for you."

I board and take my seat.

As a novice traveller, I used to like the window seat. Later on, I began to book seats on the aisle, near the washroom. My impatience gets me in the gut.

The plane is full of businessmen and businesswomen, every one of them with a head buried in some daily newspaper. I don't read newspapers for pleasure. I skim them in the morning, while sipping my grapefruit juice, and never linger for more than twenty minutes in the pages. Just long enough to find out how yesterday went for the rest of the world. It's clear that humanity is coming to an end; I'm not proud of the fact, seeing as I'm partially responsible, in my own little way, for its demise.

Tomorrow, will they be talking about the robbery at the Koreans' store? I doubt it. A robbery, a murder, this kind of thing doesn't make the headlines.

I pull a book from my bag. *Sperm Wars*, by Robin Baker. I'll pick up anything, anywhere. I prefer autobiographies to novels. I don't like fiction. I don't like people telling me stories. I want to hear the texture of the writer's voice, and there are so few true voices to be heard in books published in North America.

My own little peccadillo is research. Too many people produce prefabricated narratives that leave me cold. I have a weakness for error and imperfection. The fable of whatchamacallit dates people pretty quickly. Boredom sets in around page 32. I spend lots of pennies on novels, but few of them seduce me. I forget them as soon as I finish reading them. Even the best ones, the masterpieces, leave me unsatisfied. I want more. Novelists exasperate me.

The novelist pokes his finger in all kinds of places, searching in vain for the G-spot. The essayist, on the other hand, gets it on the first prod. No problem.

I also have a weak spot for poets. It's my Gräfenberg spot. Is that where the idea of the climax in the story comes from?

Reading is like plugging into a socket. Turning on. That's the pleasure of it.

Sometimes, film suffers from the same disease as novels – of telling too many stories. There was a time when films seemed to want to stop time in movie theatres, wanted to give people time to reflect on the images projected on the screen.

Today, the new craze is to recount the event following neoclassical narrative patterns. It drives me crazy. There's a reason I end up out of work so often.

Producers call me to shoot a series about some incident, usually a criminal one. The crimes that capture my imagination are few and far between, as are the stories about criminals that move me. What I'm looking for is the baroque and chaotic side of a criminal's life.

Being mediocre myself, I see mediocrity everywhere. I bite into the apple a stewardess has put in front of me. It's green, bitter.

My neighbour, a woman in her sixties, tears her croissant. She's surprised I haven't been given one.

"I asked for a vegetarian breakfast."

She murmurs "ah" and leans towards me, whispering that she really liked *Sperm Wars*.

"The scientist has a fascinating biological theory."

"I'm surprised that you enjoyed the book. I mean, as a woman . . ."

"The author tells us in the introduction that a lot of women will find his ideas controversial. It's true. That doesn't spoil their charm. To say that seduction is ruled by concerns of the survival of the species upsets our way of looking at male-female relationships. Not to mention female-female and male-male relationships, for that matter! When I consider my own life, it seems that Dr. Baker is completely right. I seduced my husband by following rules that were completely different from the things that led me to my lovers. I have a man who's guaranteed to protect me and another to satisfy my sexual needs . . . My comments don't shock you, do they?"

"Not at all. Quite the contrary. I was beginning to think people weren't very original. You, on the other hand, are quite the exception!"

"The other day," she says, "I read an odd piece of graffiti in the washroom of a skyscraper on Bay Street. 'If you think it's hot today, wait until you get to Hell.' It made me smile. I couldn't live with a man like the kind you see in this airplane. It might not be wise to talk this way, but it's the truth. It's my truth. I gave my all to be happy in my suburban mansion, my husband with his van, and me with my big car, our children enlisted in the best private schools in the province. Yes, enlisted is the right word! I'd gotten used to pacing up and down in the same neighbourhood over the last twenty-five years. One day, my husband went away on a business trip, and I started gobbling sleeping pills like candy. If it hadn't been for my neighbour, who plays bridge with me every afternoon at tea time, who knows? I, this little Woodbridge showpiece, might have ended up in a six-foot-long hole instead of sitting here bragging about surviving the monotony of a well-ordered existence. It was at the hospital, during my recovery, that a doctor lent me his copy of *Sperm Wars*. I saw it sticking out of his lab coat pocket and I grabbed it. The title made me laugh. 'It's a fascinating book, hypnotic,' he whispered to me. I read it straight through. Every Christmas, I buy several copies of the book and wrap them up for my friends, instead of buying them a place setting the way I used to. No, it's not the book that helped me separate from my husband. I'm talking to you about the book because it was there for me through all my tribulations."

She smiles as though we were sharing a private joke. I didn't know quite how to respond.

"I talk too much, don't I? I should have let you get a word in edgewise. Too bad we're already in Dorval. Do you know Montreal well?"

"I was born here."

"I'm going to spend a few days with my twin sister. She's a nun."

We stand up and make our way into the aisle.

"Religion," continues the woman, "there's nothing like religion. It's the only thing for which you get nothing for your money. Someone sticks out his hand to you and you empty your pockets into it. He doesn't give you anything back. Sometimes the offering boxes are so big they could be columns holding up the church."

I laugh, and hold out my hand.

She says, joking, "I don't have any money to give you. What a pleasure to meet you, Mr. Psychiatrist. You're a good listener."

I examine her shoes, and lament the fact I don't have enough time to savour her ankles.

Certain men lust after eyes, others breasts or bottoms. For me, it's ankles.

François Truffaut said that women's legs are like compass points circling the globe.

Going a whole day without leering at women's ankles is a day empty of fantasy.

The woman disappears into the crowd that pushes out the doors when we get to the airport.

I want to run after her. I don't know where to look for her, in what direction, down which hallway. She's slipped away. I stop to put the book back into my bag and, when I raise my eyes, I catch sight of Peter, my brother-in-law, going through a sliding door. He hails a taxi.

He must have been on the same airplane as I was. I'm surprised I didn't notice him before now. I smile: there he is, right after his holdup, wearing a suit and tie, looking like any ordinary businessman.

And I look like an insomniac vagrant, scatterbrained to boot. Who do I take myself for, wandering around with my sperm book?

13

T. or M. Make your choice!

Living with T. is like living in another country. Nothing like M., except the colour of money.

"Do you miss M.?"

There isn't a day that goes by without someone asking me that question.

After all these years of living with T., I've realized it's crazy to compare them.

What's red in one city is red in another.

I was born with M. I love M., even when I detest her. I grew up and became an adult with M.

I left M. to take refuge with T.

What we gain is never as beautiful as what we lose. The present is less beautiful than the past. But I don't want to talk about the past.

T. is what she is: conservative, decadent, rich. People often exclaim that she's different than she used to be. It's true that I myself have noticed this change for the better.

If T. undoes her belt, she doesn't lose her pants. She is more of a voyeur than an exhibitionist. She asks for everything and never says thank you.

It's true that T. is puritanical. She's what sexologists would label "pre-orgasmic." In other words, she's always a few seconds away from attaining a pleasure she's never known.

She's unaware of her own sensitive points.

T. has many virtues.

Beautiful, grandiose, elegant, distinguished, T. is a great, multicultural metropolis. The future of our country resembles T. more than it does M., who is often quite provincial.

T. loves to take on the airs of a reserved businessman. M. doesn't. M. is a teenager who has simply refused to grow up.

It's only T. who invites you, at three in the morning, after gallivanting around, not to have a glass of cognac, but to discuss the best way to invest your money.

T. seduces and is offended if you respond to her advances.

T. moves in a way that leaves you standing there with your mouth open. T. harasses, pursues unrelentingly.

When T. invites people to a referendum, she does it knowing full well that the results will be meaningless. If the vast majority votes "yes," the answer will be "no."

M. bends over backwards to please minorities.

T., whose lovers are generally from ethnic groups, declares outright her disgust for foreigners.

Every day, she speaks more than ninety languages. But it's in English that she's the most intimidating.

T. is the first to blow smoke in your face, when she refuses to let you smoke in restaurants.

M. looks deep into your eyes. T. never meets anyone's eye. And if she stares at you, watch out: her gaze is a call to arms.

M. warns you before pillaging your belongings. T. takes everything, pasting on her most hypocritical smile.

Wealth to one looks like poverty to the other.

No one lives with T. You can only visit T., and then you dig your way back to the next suburb.

Everyone sleeps with M.

T.'s people say, "If you want to enjoy yourself, take the plane and fly off to M."

M.'s people say, "If you want to get rich, go and see T."

When T. falls asleep, M. gets dressed to go out dancing.

I'm indebted to T. for the woman I love and our little girl, neither of whom would be in my life if I had continued to live with M.

Never say never.

A day of epiphanies. Montreal, my hometown.

The event: the premiere of my latest film, *Antigone Pacifica*.

For some reason, the organizers of the World Film Festival insist on having me meet the media. I don't know why. Obviously, the queen muse has it in for me.

The press room is on the mezzanine of a grand hotel downtown. I stop short, struck by anxiety, in the middle of the entryway, watching the comings and goings of the big players in the film industry. Everywhere there are women and men with black briefcases, directed by the radar of success. They're all chasing the big box-office hits.

Critics are anthropologists that dig into the ground, hoping to pull out some magic bone that will lift them up above anonymity and turn them into instant winners of wealth.

With my back against the wall, I feel less important than the bones of a skunk hit by a car speeding down the highway.

There are only four people in the room: Sandrine Turgeon, the journalist, adjusting the microphones; a woman in her thirties underlining a few words in the festival program booklet with thick marker strokes; an African-American student reading Stephen King's *On Writing*; and, sitting near a window with the curtains pulled shut, Thomas.

I'm thrilled to see him. It has been years. His head is buried in a newspaper folded in half on the empty seat in front of him. He's not reading. Thomas is snoozing, which explains why he doesn't look at me when I sit down next to Sandrine Turgeon.

She spreads her papers out over the surface of the table. I sneeze. I tell her it's a real pleasure to see her again. Sandrine once let me use her voice for the soundtrack on one of my documentaries.

"Do I really have to stay? The air conditioner bothers me."

"I can't do anything about the artificial air. We liked your film."

"From the back of the theatre, I could hear someone whistle," says Thomas, opening his eyes.

No one in the room reacts to his comment.

Sandrine leans over towards me: "Never mind. Your film was sheer magic!"

"Thank you. More magical than a brick wall, I hope?" I say, pulling my chair closer to the table and putting my black bag underneath it.

Thomas makes a hand gesture to tell me he'll talk to me later, after the press conference.

Sandrine pulls herself upright in her chair. I tell her that Thomas is a good friend. She begins, "I'd like to thank Fabrizio Notte for coming and talking to us this morning about his latest film. He just got into Toronto a short while ago."

I thank Sandrine, who immediately asks me about how the idea for my feature-length film originated.

I try to describe, rather unsuccessfully, I'm afraid, the source of this film on Antigone. It seems to me that nothing in the world is as boring as talking about one's work. When I finish a film, I don't even want to see it anymore, and I certainly don't talk about it to anyone.

"It took me a long time to finish this film. But I think that what you've just seen is an experiment. It's not a film.

I've tried to follow the life of a businesswoman who hasn't been too successful. It's not the story of a political refugee that a racist government throws into prison. No, that's not it. I wanted to show what life is like for a woman who spends the whole day walking, covering twenty kilometres on foot. Any walk is symbolic and, in the end, I hope she's come to a better understanding of herself. It's a walk towards love, *la marche à l'amour,* as the poet Gaston Miron wrote, is a walk into awareness, identity. She isn't from any country in particular, doesn't have any mother tongue, doesn't belong to a political party. I ask North American viewers to believe that the film is in Italian. For European audiences, I want the film to be in Arabic or Mandarin. I want every single person in the audience to feel far away from his or her homeland. Everybody. So they can grasp the sensation of being out of place that this woman lives with. She doesn't have any branch to perch on, and so she ends up falling and shattering her life."

I hear a sigh of collective exasperation in the room. My film isn't anything like what I've just described, and I know it.

The woman, a critic, barely lifts her index finger. "Mr. Notte, you are wrong to lack confidence. Your irony barely camouflages your doubts. Personally, I like your film. Your cinematography reflects our society. The fact that your work hasn't been widely reviewed is unfortunate. Believe me, you are talked about in bars and colleges. The man in the street values your artwork."

The compassion of these remarks takes me by surprise. I tell her that "artwork" is a pretty big word to describe two or three experiments.

The young student stands up: "I don't agree with your sarcasm either. You're too negative. There's nobody in this country who's dared give the subject of multiculturalism the treatment you have. Your insights are sharp, and your work cuts right to the chase. You shake people out of their complacency. In my opinion, that's a good thing."

The student searches for a metaphor while he stares at the open curtains framing the window. He thinks, scratches his head, and then turns towards me, grimacing: "You're like a trumpet player who can't stop criticizing the trumpet. Instead of singing the praises of your form, your tool, you ridicule it. It's unacceptable."

I laugh bitterly. I look pleadingly at Sandrine, who sticks the microphone under my nose.

"You're right. I have no right to criticize the tool that allows me to express myself artistically. It's stupid arrogance on my part, and I don't want to be disloyal. What I believe I want to accomplish in my films has nothing to do with it. I can't judge what they do. I'm the worst judge of my own work, even if I try to be aware of what I'm doing every second. You know, there's an actor who's pretty well known in Quebec who refused to act in this film. I won't mention any names, out of politeness, but believe me – I'm tempted! Just to put a bit of a spark into this discussion of quality. You have to watch it when you ridicule somebody well known in public, because you never know if his brother or sister is sitting in the room. At any rate, this big actor told me he would be ashamed to put his body into this film. It's important to put things into perspective. Film is, after all, only a tool. It isn't without its faults or limitations. You can choose not to like what is made in Hollywood. You can say you don't understand what films made in India are all about. You have to find something genuine in even the worst films."

"Fabrizio, do you believe your film can help save this city?"

It's Thomas who's speaking.

Everyone turns around to get a look at him. They stare at him.

Thomas moves towards the table, until he's only a couple of steps from where Sandrine and I are sitting. From our position, he looks taller, more intimidating, than he really is. His face is twisted into a wry smile.

I can feel myself getting hot under the collar, as if I'm developing a fever. I know where Thomas is headed with this. I can read his body language. It comes from arguing with him over the years.

Thomas is trying to derail the train of my thought. I'm trying to dodge his attacks.

"Film, and not just film, is all about editing. How it's put together. How can you harmonize all the separate pieces into a whole? You do it by connecting shots, scenes, sequences that weren't really meant to be put together. You have to know how to choose. That's not always easy. It's as though someone asked you to choose between your wife and your mistress. The decision is rarely made blindly. I sometimes go by my guts, act out of passion, when no other alternative seems possible. Other times, I trip onto the right trail by accident. The important thing is to show reality with as much clarity as you can muster. At every instant, I have to be perfectly lucid. I think I've achieved what I set out to do."

"I know, Fabrizio. This isn't the time to talk politics. Still, you know, there is invariably some sort of politics hiding out, playing in the background of this film. Personally, I didn't like *Antigone Pacifica* at all. It's drab. One dimensional. Blatantly self-righteous. You want to teach us something serious, but we end up leaving the theatre feeling angry, because we've been had. There's nothing deep in your images. It's really just Hollywood Canadian style. It isn't maple syrup, but it's like dry mustard with an awful lot of honey mixed into it. Just like the commercial blends you can find in any big supermarket."

These words, filled with nastiness, strike me like a fist. I'm flabbergasted. I want to grab Thomas by the collar and throw him against the wall.

I want to get out of the press room and hide somewhere, so I won't have to face this friend who just violated the cozy civility of this kind of occasion, designed to help artists and critics pass the time rather than reveal their deepest secrets to each other.

We've entered into the realm of indiscretion and bad taste. I don't want to argue in public because of an injury that was delivered somewhere else, in another context. And it is certainly a real injury.

I really thought we'd solved our problem a long time before this.

Obviously, that isn't the case. Thomas still bears a grudge towards me. He's trying to get back at me, then and there, in front of the whole world. I would never do such a thing.

"Thomas, your comments trouble me. You don't like my film. Okay. But why are you directing your anger towards me here, in front of the media?"

Thomas grimaces, as he tends to do when he objects to something that has just been said.

"Let's go out and have a drink, Thomas."

"You've turned out exactly as I predicted. You're a go-getter. You make the kind of films that will help you get ahead, with the kind of messages people like to hear. Commercials, almost. Have you listened to yourself lately? Who do you think you are?"

I'm surprised he hasn't mentioned Ada yet, because it's usually when he's with Ada that he tries to put me down like this. I refuse to give in to his criticisms.

Thomas isn't exactly the nicest kind of friend to have around. His coldness and his existential crises border on

49

mockery. I never know when he's kidding. He's a good actor. Sometimes he likes to dramatize, or create tragedy.

I stand up to go and intend to give him a hug, to try to soften the tension. But it's too late; Thomas is already halfway out the door. He disappears.

The woman critic coughs. The student yawns. Everyone abhors this sort of scene, abhors Thomas's cruelty.

Sandrine finally does something to clear the air. She says, "Someone who saw your film came by, earlier, to talk to you. Since you hadn't arrived, she left her card."

She pulls a business card from among her festival program notes, and holds it up near the microphone. *Marise Therrien, Solicitor.*

15

The last time I talked to her was at the beginning of the 1980s, more than twenty years ago, now.

On the back of her business card, she wrote in red ink: *I'm proud of you.*

I've always been careful not to talk about Marise Therrien. I don't know why. There isn't a single day that goes by without my thoughts flying off in her direction. All the women I've ever desired, all the ones I've ever loved, all, in their own way, are like Marise. If I've desired them, loved them, it's because they each incarnate some aspect of this woman I was madly in love with, when I was a teenager.

I'm insistent. I absolutely must not phone Marise. Is this a vague promise I don't need to take seriously?

Marise is an urban peasant, born in a field in Sainte-Hyacinthe. She's everything I'm not.

My stubbornness in the face of certainty remains a mystery with which I continue to annoy my therapist. I've come to the conclusion that a single god, if he exists, would not be wise enough to grasp the complexity of the human technologies that we have become.

How can we, through our spirituality, illumine our inadequacy, this inability to understand the meaning of our blindness? It's as useless as making fun of a young madman who throws himself against the windows of doors he can't see. The dust isn't really settling in my brain.

Sometimes, at night, I'm torn apart by a fundamental angst. In the daylight, I can get by, it's all right. Once the sun goes down, though, countless worries, real and imagined afflictions, set off my alarm system. My ghosts haunt me and shake me awake.

Even though my room is empty, far away from Ada's room and Rasa's, I'm sweating. I'm cloistered in my attic room that I've converted into an artificial glass paradise. Everywhere, there are windows and skylights, a well of light that never dims, not even at night. It's the light that shines through the night that hurts the most.

For the last fifteen years or so, night frightens me. I used to be a night owl, a raccoon that stalked the bars during the wee hours. I haven't turned into a pessimist. I'm persistent. What I mean is, I'm an incorrigible pessimist who laughs all the time.

I like to surround myself with people who know how to tell a good joke. I can fit into groups of strangers who share this quality, just as well as I get along with my travelling companions, just so I won't end up stuck in an impasse.

People tell me they're jealous of me because I can take off on my own for hours, in the middle of a party, a real lone ranger who doesn't share anything with anyone. Having everybody else enjoy themselves, dance, party – that's what I enjoy. Then I'm a happy man.

As far as I can tell, that's the best reason I have for choosing a profession that allows me to stay in my pyjamas all day, from early in the morning until late at night, in front of my computer, writing or correcting scripts my colleagues have written.

Yet anxiety reigns over me. I can feel it, there, a physical sensation like a metallic membrane over my whole being.

At night, I wake up because of some dream in which I'm stabbed by another me, caught in a psychological duel with myself from which I can't escape. I console myself by murmuring that I have nothing to hide, that I'm like an open book, a paperback the bookseller has torn the cover off of to send it back to the publisher. I'm the novel that doesn't sell, that no reader bothers to read.

I know that I am, paradoxically, fulfilled. I have a rich, satisfying existence. And besides – for the last few years I really haven't given a damn about having a career as an artist. I could die tomorrow and the world wouldn't stop turning. My indifference about my own life has become one of my strongest qualities.

People keep telling me I'm not an ordinary guy. I don't understand why they harp on that idea. I don't get it at all.

16

Is that the reason I get married and divorce every six years?

We've been living together, Ada and I, for almost ten years now.

I've been married three times: Bianca, Trisa, and Ada. I get dizzy just thinking about my wives.

I forget most of the lovely and not-so-lovely moments I've made happen, in order to be able to be quite content.

I love those women who have enjoyed spending a few months with a man who's hard to live with.

Marriage has never scared me off. Getting married is a contract that certain forms of love require. Either you love a friend, or you get married so that society sanctifies that love.

Marriage, however, is not a guarantee of longevity. At best, it should look like a building with windows and doors wide open. Every marriage benefits from a refreshing draught.

One morning, all of a sudden, the window breaks and the body takes off like a hummingbird on fresh green wings. It's no one's fault that the cage is broken. There's no point blaming anyone. There's no point criticizing or holding someone at fault for betraying you. And there's no point, either, in tearing someone's face apart or pulling out anyone's hair. There's nothing that can be done; it would just be lover's blackmail if you tried to stop it from happening. At some point it's time to leave, temporarily, permanently, for a day, forever. It's better to divorce on the chance that you'll remarry later on. Separation is as inevitable as marriage.

I've been divorced four times. Three times from Bianca: once by the government of Canada, another time by the government of Italy, and a third time by the Pope.

I wanted to put to rest this affair that lasted barely six months at the end of the 1970s. The inconvenient part of it was that this passion haunted me for almost twenty years. And it cost me thousands of dollars to finally put the marriage out of its misery.

One summer day, the *carabinieri* came knocking at my aunt's door, in Lanciano, when my second wife Trisa and I were visiting her.

"Who is Bianca Lopez?" the *carabiniere* demanded.

"Why?"

"Our computers show that Bianca Lopez is your wife."

"That's ridiculous. We've been divorced for twenty years."

"We'd like to believe you, but in the eyes of Italian law – and you, Mr. Notte, you are a citizen of Italy, too, aren't you? – Bianca Lopez remains your lawful spouse."

"My wife? I'm married to Trisa O'Meara."

"Trisa O'Meara?"

"My wife."

"Your wife?"

"Yes, my wife. We're here on our honeymoon."

"Then there's a problem, Mr. Notte. A rather serious problem. You are a bigamist."

The *carabiniere,* victorious, pulled on his mustache.

"A bigamist?"

"You are married to two women at the same time," stammered the *carabiniere*, studying the paper he was holding. "You are married to both Bianca Lopez and Trisa O'Meara."

"I tell you that I've been legally divorced from Bianca since 1980."

"As a Canadian citizen, perhaps. That's not the issue. It's as an Italian citizen that you have two wives, Bianca and Trisa. Mr. Notte, you are a bigamist, and because bigamy is illegal in Italy, we must put you under arrest."

"Under arrest?"

The *carabiniere* then explained to me how to solve this "barbaric" problem. "Barbaric" was the word he used. I'm sure it was a deliberate attack on me, an attempt to conquer the pride I took as an Italian in Canada, holding dual citizenship.

"Every citizenship implies responsibilities, and you have acted irresponsibly."

He let me free on bail, in provisional freedom, as soon as I had promised to get legal help.

"You must, as an Italian citizen, redivorce Bianca. If not, you won't be able to come back to Europe," my Italian lawyer told me.

The lawyer charged me a reduced rate, as a friend, and I signed a cheque from my Montreal bank account.

It took six years of mail going back and forth before I finally obtained my Italian divorce.

Free at last, I could now travel to Europe.

I'm not proud, but I don't feel guilty either.

Marriage is an integral part of my way of experiencing male-female relationships.

I love women, and I think women love me, too. No, I don't have a Don Juan complex. I feel honoured that love has knocked at my door more than once. There are so many people who never have the chance to experience love.

When my third wife, Ada, announced she was pregnant, I promised her I'd take all the necessary steps to annul my marriage before the Pope. Not that I'm a practising Catholic, I never have been, but I wanted to liberate myself from this Bianca Lopez who was nothing more than a fuzzy glow from a moment in the past.

I was hoping for a girl.

There's an odour of decomposition and stale urine around aging bachelors that repulses me. This disagreeable, fetid smell is absent from women's bodies.

As far back as I can remember, women have dragged me out of my male stupour.

Suffering from insomnia protects me from the stupidity that curses so many distinguished men. I'm a man, that's it, and I'm happy about it.

Notwithstanding this inane and finicky tautology – I'm a man, yes, and so? – it's logical that I am, myself, afflicted with the incapacity to distinguish the true from the false.

Is this why I quite impetuously choose the wrong life partner?

Whenever there are two women in a large room, I always seem to head straight for the one who will do me the most harm.

17

I'm walking in an underground shopping centre down-town. I don't really know what time it is – noon, maybe?

To avoid getting there late, I set all my watches about a half hour ahead, give or take a few minutes. It never actu-ally works to keep me on time. I'm always late.

The shopping centre is packed. On the doors of several of the stores, there are signs: "Back in fifteen minutes." Since I don't drink coffee, I don't know what I'm doing in this modern cave, but I'm pacing like a caged lion.

I'm hungry. I'm not hungry. To tell the truth, I want a martini. I'm trying to convince myself it's too early to drink anything when, suddenly, in the middle of bargaining with my willpower, I'm interrupted by an old man with a mouth like a chicken's rear who stops short a few feet away from me. He plants his feet on the floor and says hello.

I nod respectfully. He's as old as my great-grandfather and I owe him my respect. He beckons me over, and I fig-ure he's an old neighbour, someone from the same Montreal neighbourhood I'm from. After all, I lived in the city for forty years. But no; that's not it. His face isn't even familiar. He's really a stranger making wild gestures so that I'll follow him.

The old man winks at me, and since I don't budge, he walks towards me, slowly, swinging his gaze to the left and right as he walks down the hallway. I follow him, without having the slightest clue why. He positions himself in front of me, and says, "The men's washroom. Come."

"To pee?" I ask, innocently.

"To screw."

He isn't smiling. It isn't a joke.

"So I can suck your cock."

"No, thank you," I tell him, "I'm not into that."

"You've never tried. You'd like it. Only men know how to suck."

"In the washroom? Personally, I prefer beds."

"I can't. My wife's at home."

"Your wife? My! Now there's a good idea."

He doesn't get the joke.

"Screwing your wife. That works out just fine. I like older women."

"You're nuts."

"I'm not nuts. I like older women, that's all."

"Why are you roaming around here then? Who were you waiting for?"

"I'm waiting for the record shop to open. I need some CDs."

"You're not cruising?"

"Cruising? No, I don't go for men."

"As lovers?"

"I tried it when I was young and I didn't like it. I'm a cyprine guy, if you know what I mean. After the goddess-es."

"Don't try anymore. You're going to like it. You'll like it so much you'll end up like me, wandering around shopping centres talking to good-looking strangers like you."

"*In bocca al lupo*. Into the wolf's mouth. That means 'good luck' in Italian. It was a pleasure to meet you. I hope I didn't hurt your feelings."

I touch him gently on the shoulder. Under my fingers, I can feel the man's fragility, his body that seems to age with every second that passes, becoming more frail than he seemed a few minutes ago when he walked down the other side of the hallway.

The man leaves.

The window of the record shop has the usual ads for new stock. There is still no one behind the counter.

A person who doesn't question his or her sexuality, at one time or another, should be avoided at all costs. Sexuality, like identity, can't be carved in stone. I'm not born the person I am, I become it.

Nothing is more frightful than sexual fascism.

This dilettantism is my philosophy of life, and it's made it possible to get through a good part of my existence without too many bumpy patches. As many women as men have solicited me for sexual favours.

If I've sometimes refused a stranger, it was often because of a bizarre sense of being faithful to myself. Brief passages of lukewarm morality can create serious problems for me. I want to avoid unnecessary pain, things like: meeting a woman who tells you she really appreciates the intimate moments she spent with you, when there was never any sex.

That doesn't mean my sexual conduct is beyond reproach. I sometimes regret having declined an invitation. To defend a position I took yesterday, I persuade myself that a particular situation would have been improper. My refusal isn't actually based on an evaluation of the person's quality, but rather how workable the actual opportunity is to me in the particular circumstances in which I find myself.

When the right occasion presents itself – rather rarely, I must say – I accept without any second thoughts. My state of mind lends itself to this leap into the marvellous experience of ephemeral and serious passion. The promise of a mutual moment of pleasure ravishes me; the possibility of a one-way street of sensuality is enough to deflate my balloon.

As far as sex with a man goes, my humour has had to rescue me more than once from a more than slightly embarrassing expectation. You have to like the taste of blood and ammonia. I don't.

Sublimating what is authentic is at the base of psychic trauma. I prefer to take reality by the horns and throw it down on the ground of conscience rather than write disclaimers. I don't refrain from speaking up when the time is right. In fact, I talk loudly and laugh even more loudly at inappropriate times, too.

People try to hush me or get me to stop laughing. Impossible. Very quickly, my father taught me that a well-placed word could defend me as well as the blow of a fist. My enemies are struck with lashes of my tongue. I punish with carefully dealt verbal blows.

As youngsters, Thomas and I often took shortcuts on our bicycles through abandoned fields, on the northern tip of the island, where Saint-Léonard is located today. One day we came across a man who began playing with himself when he saw us coming.

"Did you see that?" I cried.

Thomas didn't see anything. I didn't believe it.

For a long time I told myself that this pervert incident was a figment of my imagination, a fantasy of my unconscious. How could it be that Thomas didn't see the exhibitionist? It seemed impossible. Either Thomas had seen him and was lying to hide the truth, or else what he said was the truth, since there was nothing strange to be seen that day.

I didn't know what to believe, how to believe anything. A discovery, like a confession, can be demoralizing.

I take my mobile phone out of my bag. I take Marise's business card out of *Sperm Wars*, where I had carefully put it, like a bookmark. What could she possibly want from me, after all these years?

I don't have the courage to call her.

I recognize the existence of the beast within me. I know that the animal will surge from my body, famished, as soon as the opportunity presents itself. Sometimes the lion in me is so wild that I can't restrain him.

I can't even count the number of mistakes I've made. So now I'm trying to learn to be a bit more careful with my passion.

It's odd that I decided to subdue this part of my prehistory with a pulp-fiction morality.

How many idiotic things do I have to put up with before I throw in the towel?

My bag of failure is starting to get heavy, and I'm sick of carrying it around me everywhere I go.

I finally make my way into the record shop. I head for the back of the store where the rock musicians whose names start with the letters D to K are stored.

I perk up at the sight of the latest album by King Crimson.

Robert Fripp.

It's rare that a musician that popular is so humble. His civility and respect for the audience is a real gift. Fripp is, however, a marginal commodity, a bit of a fringe product, a cult hit.

The sale of fringe products is the future of our cultural universe. Each of us is now a specialist. Specialization isn't meant as an insult here. A specialist is the kind of filmmaker I'm dreaming of becoming. Free. Independent. In control of the sales of my own films.

What difference can it possibly make to me to know that a man can land on Mars? The precise angle of his flight has nothing to do with saving the world. In any case, not Earth.

You have to know who's got his finger on the trigger, because capitalism has never had a pretty face. You want to become a nobody, not a success.

I sit down on a bar stool at Boccaccio, in the Hôtel Bonaventure. I've been coming here since the 1970s. Nobody ever wants to join me here for a glass of wine. People don't think it's cool enough for them. What kind of person comes to this kind of lounge? Tourists and businessmen. What's wrong with that? And yet most of the writers I admire have spent a good part of their lives in hotels.

I light a cigarette. I feel worse than a hit-man, because I'm aware that the smoke from my cigarette will eventually kill every customer in this room. I take a puff or two before crushing the butt in an ashtray.

"You may smoke here," the bartender tells me politely, with a French accent.

"I feel guilty enough as it is, thanks," I say in French. "I think I'll pass. I'll smoke later on, outside. Could you please get me a cheese sandwich and a glass of red wine?"

My taste for tobacco came on me suddenly, at twenty-seven years of age, in Mexico. I was living there with Bianca. I had to do something to fill my time, in the long empty days between bouts of feverish activity.

I came to enjoy living in that monstrous city that never sleeps. The breathtaking rhythm of uninterrupted, unrelenting urban life. Life, twenty-four seven, anywhere and everywhere. More than twenty million men and women bumping into each other on the frenetic boulevards of Mexico City. México, Distrito Federal. I was dizzy twenty-four hours a day, spinning around in an ever-moving Eldorado. Everything within reach, everything at the right distance.

Actually, I started to enjoy having a cigarette once in a while when Bianca fell for Armando. Within four months,

I was smoking more than a pack a day. That's how worrisome their passion was for me. It only took a brief moment of distraction for me to lose Bianca.

It was too ridiculous to cry over and too loony to get angry about. I don't lament the loss. Not anymore. I don't think the separation threw me too far off course. When it's over, it's over. I don't like obsessing, and certainly don't want to beg for love. It's disgusting to see what we'll do when we are prisoners of our emotions.

Being twenty-five years old and worshipping Biana, this is what Mexico means to me.

Today I'm forty-eight years old and I worship Ada. That's what Toronto means to me.

Between these two poles there's Trisa.

I didn't drown in mad love with Trisa. Our love was reasonable. It should have stayed in the companionship phase. We both abused our mutual seduction which finally played a dirty trick on us.

Anger in a couple needs to be maintained at a reasonable level, or you risk shaking the very foundation of your passion. Trisa and I both took the risk and, as a result, we both lost everything. Up in smoke.

I love them all: the all-woman woman, who doesn't have a fingernail of masculinity; the solid, stable woman who has both feminine and masculine qualities; and the masculine woman whose only feminine trait is her sex. I love women because they open the eyes of the frustrated man I sometimes am, insensitive to the vibrations around me, mysteries that I can no longer grasp on my own.

Whether I'm in Mexico in Bianca's arms, in Montreal with Trisa, or in Toronto with Ada, I have the impression that I'm in the arms of another woman, one who is more than the woman I'm living with. The more-than-woman, you might say.

I am, therefore, an intrinsically unfaithful partner. I desire a woman who is not the one I'm with. Who is this woman I should be with?

These women are all closely connected by a fine, invisible thread. I'm the only one who can see the thin string that ties them together. I can't cut it. You don't cut what can't be broken.

18

Someone is tapping me on the shoulder. It's Thomas. At that very moment, my cell phone rings. I motion to Thomas to excuse me.

Sandrine Turgeon tells me she won't be joining me; she's sorry, but she has to stay where she is, miserable, because she has appointments she can't postpone. I thank her profusely for her kindness.

Without the fierce happiness of people who are open and inspiring, like Sandrine Turgeon, life would be dull. Nothing distracts them from the road hammered down by the rush towards communal well-being. If she hadn't been at the press conference, I would have left.

Thomas sits down on the stool to the right of me.

"I knew I'd find you here."

"It's been more than ten years since I've set foot in the place."

"You can't teach an old monkey to grimace. I wasn't very courteous a few minutes ago. I'm not going to apologize, because I think what I said was true. But I need to learn some manners."

I remember that one night in particular, after swallowing some LSD pills, he took his father's hunting rifle out of the cabinet and pointed it towards my forehead.

Was he joking? I'm not sure.

Every time I cried for help he lowered it and caressed it, and as soon as I calmed down he raised it to my head again. It was the worst *bad trip* ever.

Thanks to Thomas, I never bothered with psychedelic travels after that.

I don't know what comes over me. I'm delighted to see Thomas. I tell him I shiver with pleasure when I think that I'm managing to get by all right living with Ada.

It's not easy harmony. I admit we've failed to stay on key sometimes. Still, in the last few months, I've started to understand what Ada's pragmatism brings to our relationship.

As a teenager, I used possess great quantities of idealism. After a while, after negotiating with other people, my idealism turned into something more tangible free from cynicism.

Ada is cold-blooded. Few people are as gifted at being firm as she is. Tough-minded, even. She has unearthed the key that was buried who knows where, and has opened the doors of satisfaction and satiety.

I'm thrilled that Ada chose me. She didn't need a man in her life. Her autonomy is astonishing. My heart leaps every time she asks me how I am. She doesn't need my knowledge and so if, in the morning, she wheedles me into doing her some favour, I turn on like a household appliance.

Our conversations are rarely easygoing. The calmness can collapse in a heap without a second's notice. Nothing is more fragile than a male's usefulness. A man doesn't count for much in a woman's life, these days. If he matters at all, it's always for some precarious reason.

This confession is not intended to be a defence of women to the detriment of the male. It would be idiotic for me to lower myself by publicly humiliating men.

I am for women. I fight for the cause of women's freedom. I'm, of course, kidding when I call myself a lesbian. I like making love with her, it's as simple as that.

Slavery persists in every human domain, including that of the emotions. As I go on living with Ada, I've come to feel that emotions don't stir me much, even if she often reproaches me for my sentimentality.

Coming from her, this condemnation is beyond my grasp. Isn't it Ada, this doctor of the body, who taught me that emotions are a fabrication of the mind, like cellular phones or transcendental subjects?

I've started to mistrust easy tears. I try to make myself impermeable to leaky states of mind. Ada claims that reason remains the only way to get from point A to point B. Reprimands must be neither hyper-emotional or phlegmatic. The perfect balance weighing in on our judgment.

The only escape valve is presence, self-awareness, irrepressible outpouring of laughter. The man who laughs dips his hands into tides forgotten by the lightning rod. Ada laughs all the time.

I'm jealous of people who make her laugh.

For Thomas, fake laughter comes easy. He is naturally witty.

One summer, Thomas fell in love with Ada.

In a way, he was helping her out. I had made her swallow a heavy dose of misery, apparently. That summer, Ada and I rented a cottage on Georgian Bay. Thomas's wife had just left him for a nurse, the woman she worked on the night shift with.

Thomas fell to pieces. He knocking back rum and cokes by the bottleful.

One day I ran into him on Saint-Denis, while on a quick trip to Montreal. I was synchronizing the soundtrack for a documentary on the mafia. He was unrecognizable. He had lost at least ten kilos and started growing a beard. This man, who so hated jackets and cigars, was wearing a tuxedo and smoking a Cohibo.

I felt like crying when I saw him there, sitting in a bar, looking like a bum and cursing the world for making him miserable. Despite looking very distinguished, he was pathetic, a smart-suited businessman, elegant and drunk.

I convinced him to come and spend a few weeks in the sun with Ada and me. Rasa wasn't born yet.

Thomas agreed.

He took an extended leave from his job, as owner, chief cook and bottle-washer at a brand-name men's furnishings store, and moved into the cottage.

In the days to come, he gained back some of his weight – Ada was a consummate chef – and eventually decided to shave his beard. He folded up his jacket in a plastic cleaners' bag and started wearing jeans again.

Every afternoon, while I edited my film about hired killers, he had long conversations with Ada who, neglected by my need to work, was eager for company.

From sentence to sentence, paragraph to paragraph, laugh to laugh, words were transfigured into gestures which, in turn, extended into caresses, right up to the point where I caught them in Ada's bed. She was in the middle of eating him, she who abhorred fellatio.

I don't remember who said that a wife finds pleasure with her lover doing the things that she detests doing with her husband, but he was right. I was stunned.

I leapt out of the room and went for a walk on the beach, twisted by a physical pain that was as excruciating as the suffering I felt in my childhood when I was hit on the head with a baseball bat.

Curiously, I suffered more in my body than in my mind. It was as though my heart revolted against the evidence. Only my body was wounded by the blow. In the end, I came back and sat down at the table to eat with Ada and Thomas. I never mentioned what had happened.

It would have been useless to protest, or even to stand up and break Thomas's jaw. Not because I didn't want to.

It wouldn't have taken much to convince me to let my fist make contact with his nose.

I've never figured out what made me persist in standing in the middle of the kitchen, listening to *Bitches Brew* by Miles Davis, turning the volume of the stereo up as loud as I could to stifle the noises that were rising up out of Ada's room.

And I stayed mute for a long, long time, too long, until the day Ada kicked Thomas out the door. In a matter-of-fact way, as though there was nothing going on between them worth mentioning, she told me she was tired of playing doctor.

Every couple that uncouples is miserable. Experts advise against sticking your nose between a man and a woman who are going through a crisis. It's too bad, because this warning ignores the other side of the coin. Everyone needs a shoulder to cry on.

Every love story finishes with a predictable, banal scene. The couple separates, one runs to the friend of the other. Often, the friend decides to console one member of the couple rather than the other, for no particular reason or need. When war breaks out and the whole thing disintegrates, what is left to be done? Just kiss the friend who saved the couple from something much worse.

The problems start when the war is over and the couple reunites. Then you're forced to condemn the friend who threw you the life jacket.

To this day, neither Ada, Thomas nor I have ever spoken about this incident. We recognize that the lessons we learn from love can't be put into words. Emotions don't speak, they just make themselves felt.

Thomas is talking. "I've given up the rat race. I've sold the clothing store. As some Italian-American said in a movie: 'Someone made me an offer I couldn't refuse.' The price was right. So here I am, an unemployed but independently wealthy man."

"You're a lucky guy to have all this free time."

"I've started painting. I scrawl with acrylic on large canvasses. It isn't very good. I like to play at being a painter."

"You don't have an ounce of artist's blood."

"Meanie."

I take a bite of my sandwich. I have trouble picturing Thomas spreading colours over a canvas with his big bear paws.

Thomas doesn't say anything, giving me time to dip the last piece of dry bread and a few French fries into the spicy mustard.

Then he continues: "I've met an extraordinary woman."

"A woman who loves you."

"She wants to have a baby. We've been trying for a year. In vain. The sperm counts show that it's my fault it's not working."

"You should have something to eat. You're starting to lose weight."

Thomas orders a steak tartare. He raises his glass of white wine.

"Let's toast your film."

"Thank you. *Sangue e latte*. Blood and milk."

"You don't need to translate. The tone of your spiel says it all. I've known you for more than a century, Fabrizio Notte."

He pulls out the Italian pronunciation of my name, exaggerates it.

I can feel his love for me in his voice.

"To your health and prosperity!" he adds, in a friendly, unassuming voice.

He takes a sip of wine, studies my face for a moment, and then: "Fabrizio, what would you say to selling me . . ."

He pulls a joint of hashish out of his linen jacket and passes it to me. "It's good stuff."

I drink my wine and examine the joint.

I sniff it and slide it into my pack of cigarettes.

"I was saying . . . I need . . . a little of your . . . sperm."

Unable to swallow the wine in my mouth, I spit a few drops into my plate. The result is disgusting. I do manage, however, to sputter out a few syllables.

"You must be kidding."

I watch him. He inspects me. Silence.

He scratches his head.

"You aren't kidding," I say, stupefied.

"We've tried everything. Linda has an appointment with a Chinese agency. She's started the process of adopting a child. I'm not convinced it's a good plan. I suffer from agoraphobia. I'm not made for great adventures."

"I'm honoured by your offer. But you know how Ada is, conservative right down to the marrow in her bones. She won't agree."

"Even if I'm the one who asks?"

"Especially if you're the one who asks, Thomas, given the history you have with her. She's been through enough with you."

"Talk to her."

Putting my glass to my lips, I try to think of some clever retort. Nothing comes to mind. There's a black hole in the middle of my brain. It's sucking up every intelligent thought I've ever had.

I don't want to be there, talking to Thomas about my sperm.

I get down off the stool.

"You leaving?"

"It's better this way, Thomas. My brain is totally blitzed."

I pay both our bills and take Thomas into my arms.

"Here's what I say: break a leg. You're going to need all the luck in the world. Listen, I have to go. They're waiting for me at the Festival."

Thomas sits back down, in front of his glass of white wine, a sombre smile twisting his face.

I emerge from the dusky bar, bowled over by the conviction that this friend has just tried to make a fool of me.

19

I'm fainting in the stifling heatwave. I certainly don't want to go back to the world of film.

Via col vento. Gone with the wind.

I light a joint on Boulevard René-Lévesque, near Rue Université. I take two drags and then put the rest of it away for later.

I don't know where I am. They've changed all the street names. The ugly, pretentious buildings stay the same.

Coming to Montreal is like poring over a high school year book.

Joy, melancholy, bodies of beautiful girls and faces of good-looking boys, happiness, sadness, hope invading me at the end of this month of August.

It's about one o'clock in the afternoon. I hail a taxi.

"*Tourist?*" the driver asks me in English.

"No, I've just had a bit too much to drink."

The Haïtian man behind the wheel laughs. "Bravo! Where are you going?"

"Saint-Laurent. Because even if I've never lived there, that street is the path through my existence. From one end to the other."

"Okay, Saint-Laurent it is then. From Saint-Antoine to Gouin, *ça va?*"

"Sure. Don't mind me if I don't talk. I'm not feeling much like conversation."

"*Il n'y a pas de quoi*. Sometimes I drive clear across the island without saying a word to my passengers. It happens to us, too, you know. Cab drivers know how to be quiet. Here, I'll turn off the radio."

"You don't need to do that," I tell him.

His finger has already pressed the button. All we can hear now is the purring of this old American engine that sputters at every red light.

Neither the high school I went to, nor my father's place is part of the adventure of Boulevard Saint-Laurent, but, all the same, there's no other street like it to light sparks of memory for me, memories that are now becoming dimmer with age.

Saint-Laurent cuts the city of Montreal in half.

I remember a poetry reading in the 1970s, where anglophone and francophone poets were invited to read from their work.

That evening, when it was my turn to read – I'd only published a chapbook of poetry at the time – I wanted to highlight the fact that I was the only Italian invited and, since I was part of neither linguistic groups officially represented there, I decided to stand in the doorway that divided the room in two. It was a way of showing them how essential I thought it was to see in the Other a symbol of difference which, in reality, synthesizes the cultural conflict that so violently separates our country.

The reason Montreal is so interesting is because it boasts a street like this one that is called Saint-Laurent.

Who is Saint Laurent?

There's no mention of him in the dictionaries I've looked in. The only Saint Laurent they talk about in history books is a politician, who was born in 1882 and died in 1973. Unlikely that this prime minister would have given his name to such a magnificent boulevard.

As with any beginning, the origins of the name are too complex to be reduced to a simple description. What matters is how this boulevard is made up of eleven emotional sections.

The first section, which I call *La Vieille*, is the old part that runs from the St. Lawrence River and ends at Saint-Antoine (once called Craig). This is where, in the 1960s, before the Autoroute Ville-Marie was built, you'd find pawnshops. This is where you'd go to buy your first camera or a new guitar. There is nothing left of stores like that these days, except for the shadow of our adolescence that lingers in all of us. Today, I have to go to Steve's to get my Gibson Lucille (autographed by B. B. King!).

In one of my albums, I have a photo of Marise, standing in front of the concrete skeleton that would later be transformed into the courthouse.

The second section of Boulevard Saint-Laurent goes from Viger to René-Lévesque: it's Chinatown. Even if it's much less extensive than Toronto's or New York's Chinatown, it's still a sacred space. Once a week I ate there, alone or with friends, at the Crystal Saigon, the Hong Kong or else the Hun Dao.

Between René-Lévesque and de Maisonneuve, you're in the third section, which I call *La zona rossa*. It's where you go to get something you don't want to admit out loud.

Farther north, between de Maisonneuve and Sherbrooke, is *Little India*. People who want to spend a few cents will be amazed at the prices charged for the merchandise there. *Little India* was, more than anything else, the Théâtre de La Licorne, where I attended the premieres of plays by Marco Micone, the first Italian playwright in the country.

It's also a bookstore called *Las Americas*, the place you can buy a novel in Spanish by the Mexican author Mónica Lavín.

Rue Saint-Norbert is engraved into the memories of women and men who fought against the demolition of the historical buildings along this magical street.

Then we come to Saint-Laurent *La Hip*. From Sherbrooke up to Rachel, people can enjoy an opportunity to forget their cares.

The old Élysée theatre, on Milton, is a landmark for me. That's where Patrick Straram le bison ravi showed the best films of the 1960s. I haven't set foot on this little street for many years. L'Élysée no longer exists.

The anarchist publisher Dimitri Roussopoulos convinces me to set up my office near Rue Prince Arthur. According to Dimitri, I'm the pluriculturalism of Saint-Laurent *par excellence*. I sign a three-year lease for a studio in the Balfour building, where we'll move our production offices.

During this time, I learn a lot about good food by visiting the endless list of restaurants nearby: Luna, Bonna Notte, the Shed and La Caféteria, or by ordering a *pannino* from Montenegro, Hoffner, or Fattouch. Among other things, I learn that a little something to eat could mean something other than a hot dog.

La Hip also has its intellectual side. Bookstores like L'Androgyne (for gay and lesbian literature) and Gallimard (for their amazing number of titles in stock) offer a selection of books that is hard to find elsewhere.

And we can't forget the Cinéma Parallèle, which would expand into l'Ex-Centris. One year, Claude Chamberland presented the complete works of the brilliant filmmaker John Cassavetes, my favourite.

North of Avenue des Pins, we arrive in the Jewish quarter. They tell me Waldman's, the fish-seller, isn't what he used to be. Could be. That's where I used to buy my calamari, when I wasn't vegetarian yet.

Another good bet: meat eaters, don't miss Schwartz's!

They serve a smoked meat sandwich nobody can beat. Sitting in front of the window, you can see L. Berson & Fils, the family business that makes tombstones for Jewish cemeteries.

And Moshé's has the best choice of kosher food. Dimitri took me there one night so I could hear his praises for the magnificent Main: "If you prefer fish, you have to go to the Portuguese place next door. And if you like blues, there's Luther Johnson playing at the Bar G-Sharp."

In fact, I went there, last winter, to hear the consummate musician play his Strat so generously, way into the wee hours of the morning. Afterwards I went to ask him to sign his CD. He didn't know how to write. He traced two Xs under his photo.

Then there are the *Indecisive* and *Intermediate* sections, between Rachel and Van Horne.

Rue Marie-Anne was made famous by Leonard Cohen and, northwest of that, Beauty's, where dozens of people stand in line every morning, patiently waiting for their breakfast. I went there, many times, with Thomas. We'd talk about our love affairs.

On the other hand, I'm crushed to see the former Bank of Montreal building, near Mont-Royal, with its glorious façade in such a state of disrepair. It's almost in ruins. And its future is in jeopardy. As a young man, a dreamer, I used to sit under its huge pillars, seducing some pretty stranger I had met in a little poets' café that has disappeared.

Just south of Laurier, there is a *bellissima* church, Saint-Enfant Jésus, with Italian arches.

At the corner of Laurier and Saint-Laurent, a fire station which was once the City Hall of the little town of Saint-Louis, which Montreal annexed in 1906.

A few steps further on, the Lux (which is no longer) was, for me, one of the most fascinating spots on this part of the street. Otherwise, this area leaves me a bit cold. The ethnic presence hasn't yet flourished here.

Soon we come to the real centre, between Van Horne and Jean-Talon, the area which has a real place in my heart. *La Petite Italie*, Little Italy.

How can I summarize this eighth section of Boulevard Saint-Laurent in a few lines?

I'm thrilled to see that the immigrants' children have been able to transform the little houses that belonged to their parents into a young, vibrant neighbourhood.

The Caffè Italia and the Milano are the cafés that non-Italians know best. The ones that attract me today are the Caffè internazionale – oh, look! It's changed names – and Cinecittà (also gone), the Libreria italiana, Dai Baffone (on Dante) and the Tre Marie (on Mozart).

You don't really know *la piccola Italia* if you don't go to see the place where I was baptized, the Madonna della Difesa, where Mussolini *il Duce* sits upon his brown horse. It's a source of ethnic shame. A statue of Dante has been erected outside, to try to make everyone forget the narrow-mindedness of Italian nationalism.

The ninth section is, basically, Jarry Park. Pope John Paul II went there, no doubt to see a good amateur soccer match. I, myself, played several games there myself during the 1980s! No, the Pope wasn't there to watch.

North of Jarry, on Rue Liège, I spent several summers working in a textile factory. It was there that, following the advice of the manager, Mr. Oronoff, I wrote my first poems. How many conversations about writing did I have with this modest man who was an expert on poetry! I owe so much to this master who knew how to be patient with a rebellious teenager and a poor worker like me.

The Metropolitaine, between Crémazie and Fleury, slices the city in half, dividing the south from the north. My parents lived in this area for a year, before they were married, in the 1950s, before the birth of my sister and me, a few yards away on Saint-Hubert.

We are getting to the industrial zone, which I have named *La Fabrique*. The tenth section of Boulevard Saint-Laurent is the one I know best, because my mother worked many long years in one of the textile factories before she retired in 1981.

On Sunday, after the family meal, my father would take me to the Rivoli Theatre, where they showed films in Italian. He took me to see the pictures starring Totò, the great Italian actor. Some day they should show the films with that genius from Naples in French.

Then we get to Saint-Laurent *La Tranquille*. The last section of the street is calm. Of all the streets in Montreal, it's Gouin I like the best. It runs along the side of the Rivière-des-Prairies, the only place in Montreal where you really have the feeling the city is an island.

The *Rive sud* has become completely commercial, ruined, while on the north side of the island, made up of individual properties, has retained its natural splendour.

I was invited, one Saturday afternoon, to a Jewish wedding which took place near the river. It was as though we had been transported to a completely different city. Listening to the Rabbi's sermon outdoors, we felt the radiant vegetation light up the silent riverbank.

I ask the taxi driver to stop. I pay my fare. I walk towards the river. The Rivière-des-Prairies isn't the Adriatic or California. It's tiny and familiar.

I sit down on a bench in front of the river and smoke the cigarette I couldn't finish at Boccaccio.

Years pass, and the names of the streets change.

I need something solid to hold on to in this vast, moving landscape that is memory.

20

My cell phone rings.

"Fabrizio, it's Marise. Sandrine Turgeon gave me your number. You weren't going to call me, were you? Well, I couldn't wait. I have to talk to you."

"I'm up to my neck in work."

"Where are you?"

"I'm not sure. A Montrealais who can't remember street names – that's gotta be pretty rare. I remember a time when I could drive through the city with my eyes closed."

"You have to forgive me. I couldn't get away from work. I had to finish tweaking a contract before noon. We'll get together later."

"I'm taking the last plane to Toronto."

"Find some way to get out of it. Please."

"I have to get back. I'm shooting a film."

"I'm going to throw myself off the Jacques-Cartier Bridge."

"Your husband left you for a younger woman? A thirty-year-old?"

"She's twenty-two."

"Come on, you'll be fine. Take some time off. Take a trip somewhere."

"Remember, it was you who told me we have to suffer to be artists. At the time, it made me sick to my stomach to hear it. I guess I'll just wait for you to call."

"Marise – I can't."

I want to shake myself and shout, "What have I got to complain about? I'm calm, my marriage has survived, I love my partner, she loves me, we have a child who is the centre of our universe and, yes, I've got a fancy car, a beautiful house. As you can see, I'm just an ordinary guy. The waves on the river hypnotize me. I'm in a trance. Somebody has stuck a gag between my jaws."

"I'll meet you at six o'clock, at Baffoni's," she insists.

I feel like singing, the way they do in musicals, "Fine" or "Thanks" or "It's my destiny to be with you" or "I'll stop making my stupid films."

Marise, do you remember *Faces* by Cassavetes? Godard, Bergman, Fellini, Olmi? They're my gods now. My idols. We can't all be the queen bees. I'm one of the crones who plods along, who doesn't do anything great, but who does it with love and sincerity.

Nothing but prosaic inanities. Certain feelings can't be translated into words.

Marise hangs up.

I hit END.

The end.

Marise Therrien. The first woman I ever loved, the one I loved more than I could ever love anyone after her. To see her again, to even touch her hand, perhaps, tentatively, as though by accident . . . this is still possible, it seems.

I run my hand across my forehead and up into my hair. Is it the heat? The cold? I can't tell hot from cold right now. Pain and pleasure have a common intensity.

I'm trembling. I'm thinking about the time Marise's chestnut hair was cropped like a boy's, in 1968, when the rest of the world had long, curly hair.

Disciplined, intelligent, athletic, hardworking, she needed to be watched in order to feel alive, and yet she never called anyone.

She hated solitude and couldn't stand to be alone with her shadow for more than fifteen minutes. Suffering horrified her. She laughed quietly and refused to cry in public. Did she ever let go, at least in private?

Her superficiality ran deep. The more Marise fooled around, the more intelligent and perceptive she became.

The fact that I was her first heartthrob meant, paradoxically, that she refused to let me become her first lover. She had saved this privilege for a Parisian who, she admitted to me later, had not properly appreciated the sweet secrets of her virginal body.

It broke my heart in two.

After being wounded this way, I made sure I would never agree to be any woman's first lover.

Not being chosen by Marise was an act of cynicism, an experience fate bestows on neophytes who court in vain, as well as an act of cruelty which only a person who really loves another can imagine.

Some years later, at the end of a brutally hot summer, long after Marise had savoured the bitter fruits of her escapades with her amazing Parisian, I invited her over to my parents', who were out dancing that night.

That first evening of love didn't produce fabulous results, given that each of us aspired to the selfish, carnal fantasies of previous lovers.

We woke up after the longed-for embrace with disappointment in our limbs. Marise fell more and more often prey to her unfounded suspicions, arising mainly out of a rejection of our cultural differences, and I became more obsessed with this unrequited love.

I would have given anything to live with Marise.

One of the last times we were together, we were thirty and found ourselves, by chance, both living in lower Westmount, in apartment buildings right across the street from each other.

I had just divorced Bianca.

Once again, instead of choosing me, Marise had taken a tall, thin guy, moderately nice, intellectually curious, and soft. She had decided, on their first date, that he would be the father of her child.

More than once, I begged her, though with unfailing subtlety, to leave the celery stalk she was with and move in with me instead. Marise didn't love me "that way."

Our relationship had risen, I thought, or fallen, Marise thought, to a level of pure and simple friendship.

She confessed that she had never really loved me.

If, the first time, when she was fourteen, she had gazed fondly on me, it was only a momentary act, done on a dare. She wanted to steal me away from her neighbour and friend, Virginie, a young girl I was going out with, who introduced me to Marise, and who, in 1990, committed suicide.

Egotism is a small-mindedness that pushes people to behave in an irrational manner. Marise had been insensitive. She had done me wrong, led me down the garden path like a baby lamb.

After so many years, though, the real question still went unanswered. Which one of us had acted more like an ungrateful so-and-so?

Marise, who had conquered me for her own base reasons of personal ambition? Or me, who had always believed that I could turn around the state of our affairs, which were clearly going in only one direction – hers?

Marise had not remained faithful to her first impulse. When she gave into it later on, at the screening of one of my films, it was clear that her impulse didn't have much to do with either love or lust. If it did, and if she had – imagine this for a moment – won her bet with herself, she would have dropped me the first night we spent together, right there, on the corner of the 15th Avenue and Villeray, in

Saint-Michel. She would have tossed me out like the wrapper from the chewing gum she popped in her mouth right after our first kiss.

It didn't happen that way. I would swear by fire that it wasn't that. Did she honestly want to leave me the first night? I refuse to believe that. If this were really the case, then would I actually be the one who was guilty of holding on to her, against her wishes, for a year and a half, singing my hurting songs and acting the part of the wounded hero? Would that make me the real monster of my nightmares? Was it possible that Marise just stayed with me out of pity?

That first evening, after our lips parted from each other, when we whispered "good night," I didn't notice any distaste or any hint of farewell.

Impossible. I couldn't have been stubborn enough to walk by her side, if she had clearly been indifferent to me. I was blinded by love, for sure, but I wasn't that self-destructive! In Marise there lay a need to be taken care of that went way beyond the companionship of puppy love. I had uncovered this neediness in her, a deep desire for affection, very early. It was there when she was fourteen, and I saw it again when she was twenty. At thirty, she was no longer taking my calls.

One night, I was overtaken by a mad wish to grab both her arms and shake her as hard as I could, not to hurt her, but to make her understand that the support she was looking for was right there before her eyes. It didn't seem to matter to me that my anger could hurt her as much as it did.

Not to have been chosen . . . that's what is at the root of all of my torments, the reason I torture myself.

God, was she beautiful!

Marise was married twice. Not to her tall, skinny celery stalk, though, although he did become the father of her first daughter.

I had no right to love her. Not because I am unworthy of her love – I deserve her love as much as any of the men she chose; I know that – but because I can't love a woman indefinitely when she has not chosen me.

No matter what I do, what I give her, in the end, she will not love me. You can't force a heart to beat for you when it doesn't want to.

I'm not proud to admit it, but, this afternoon, the naughty gnome inside me is laughing a mocking laugh.

No doubt, for the first time in her life, Marise is suffering from a broken heart.

Just like the one I had, the ones that thousands of victims of tragic love affairs have borne, Marise's broken heart has put her face-to-face with the anguish of unrequited love.

She is suffering because she loves a man who doesn't love her; she is suffering because she knows she will go on loving this man who will never love her back; she is suffering because she has just entered into the clan of victims of unrequited love.

To be shaken up so brutally, to have pain come to roost in your heart: you know that there will be someone you'll love until the day you die, someone who will never, ever be in love with you.

My entire body pulls itself straight to face the evidence. This is how it is.

I hail a taxi.

"Rue Anne-Berger, please. Near the corner of Armand-Bombardier and Maurice-Duplessis."

21

Lina arrives in Montreal in 1952, under the burning hot sun of August. Guido is at Central Station and, despite a twelve-month separation, recognizes his beloved as soon as she gets off the train. In the crush of the crowd and the luggage piled up on top of each other, Lina emerges from the steam of trains parked at the station. Guido hurries over to get her. The lovers find themselves before each other, immobilized, staring, speechless. Lina bends her knees and places her two suitcases on the ground, her eyes never leaving the man for whom she has given up her whole family.

As a good Italian man, I don't hesitate to say it: my mother is an exceptional woman. She fought to live with the man she loved. She gave up everything to follow the source of the flame burning in her heart. She walked away from her family, her security, her home; she was disowned by her brothers and her sisters.

The post-war rural existence wasn't well suited for young couples who wanted to live together. This did not stop the twenty-three-year-old woman from linking her destiny to that of a man mistrusted for his ferocious independence.

The lack of trust and respect worked both ways. Guido's family hated Lina's family. My parents were a modern-day Romeo and Juliet.

A girl and a boy insisted on swimming against the current and, after fifty years together, even in their bathing suits, they still worship each other.

Obviously, there have been good times and bad times. Over the years, their marriage has proven to the world that it was possible to share a love that respected both partners.

People have a hard time understanding how such a stable love affair could produce a child who is so unstable. Who would believe it? Because they had everything to gain, they had nothing to lose. You have to lose something to gain everything.

They shaped their own balance, without any help from anyone, building it up day by day, so that, today, they can rest comfortably. It doesn't hurt that they had a good pension plan, either. Finally, they can enjoy the fruits of their arduous labours, the sweat of their brows dripping day in, day out, in textile and steel mills.

The strange thing is, neither my father nor my mother ever complained about the daily exploitation they endured.

Lina says, philosophically, "You have to know how to walk with your head high, and not bump into the little branches along the way. Otherwise, you'll never make it to wherever you're going."

"Don't you miss Italy?" I ask.

My father answers me in French. "*Manquer quoi?* What is there to miss – rich landowners? I didn't want to be under the thumb of another Italian."

"Why didn't you ever apply to become a Canadian citizen?"

The question is not really naive. If I have the right to my Italian citizenship, it is only because they chose to remain Italians themselves.

My father continues in Italian. "I was born Italian and I will die Italian. Who I am has nothing to do with the country I live in. I'm grateful to Canada for its generosity, for having given us all these good things. This is where I want to be buried. I don't have to change my colours for that.

88

Respecting others starts with treating yourself with dignity. Without your dignity, you're nothing."

My mother is thrilled to see me behind the aluminium door. She stretches her neck out so that I'll give her kisses on each cheek. My father wipes his mouth and places the serviette on the table, then comes and joins us in the hall.

"Have you eaten?" he asks, shaking my hand.

"You're always travelling!" my mother exclaims. "Ada mustn't be too happy about that."

"I was invited to show my new film."

"Sit down," my mother says, "eat with us. It's not much. A salad with tomatoes from the garden, fried hot peppers, provolone, and bread."

I sit down at the table. My mother brings me cutlery, a plate, and a wine glass into which my father pours a bit of white table wine.

"Tell me what you think of it. It's this year's vintage."

The wine is both resinous and slightly bitter, and I say, "It reminds me of a Greek Retzina. A very good one."

"What do you expect? I come from the south of Italy. I think this is the last year I'll make wine. We only drink a glass a day, at the noon meal. With my diabetes, I hardly drink."

My father has been a diabetic since the age of sixty. His diet has now made him lose weight; he no longer looks like the sturdy man he once was. He doesn't eat much, he insists on eating at regular times; otherwise, he feels weak, faint. My father flatters himself by thinking he is in touch with his body. He talks as though he's been taking yoga courses, which is not the case.

"Fabrizio, you have to take care of your body. If you don't, you'll pay for it when you're older. You look well, healthy. Don't forget: as long as your belly doesn't hide your penis when you piss, you're doing okay."

"You've got your smile back," my mother adds. "Things are all right?"

"Yes, things are good. Except for a few reviewers who didn't like my latest film. Nobody's talking about it, and I think that silence reflects the disdain of the press. I'm beside myself. Thomas hates it. At least he's honest with me; I prefer it when critics say what they really think about what I do. Even a bad review in the newspapers is something. Better than not talking about it. The media doesn't pay much attention to independent cinema. It turns their whole system upside down."

"Just do what you have to do," my mother says.

The sun slants in between the sliding doors and catches the wine glasses. The peppers are really very hot. I have to wipe my forehead.

The breeze caresses my mother's grey hair. Overnight, she has decided to stop dyeing it.

"I like the bluish highlights in your hair," I tell her.

"I just came back from the hairdresser's. Do you like my new cut?"

"I like short hair on women."

"You've cut your hair, too," my father says. "You look younger, different. I can't remember the last time I saw you with short hair."

"I've never worn it short. I've had long hair since I was a kid. Since the Beatles."

"Personally – now don't get mad – I prefer you with long hair," my father says.

"That's strange, because we always used to fight over my long hair."

"You see, I've changed, too. Even if your mother says that I'm stubborn as a mule."

We laugh. My mother says, "I should film you. You should see how you act sometimes. You're a nut."

"I know. I'm a naughty little devil."

My father smiles. My mother directs a pointed comment at me. "How are Rasa and Ada?"

I notice the child comes first, then the mother. In fact, she talks more about my niece Eve than her mother, my sister Lucia. It must be because of that intrinsic feeling grandparents have for their future generations of descendants. I don't know.

My father would have liked to have grandsons, to ensure the family name would be carried on. But he's got used to the idea that the future is in the hands of women.

"Rasa is taking piano lessons at the Conservatory, and swimming lessons. She gave her first concert in April. Not bad, for a little five-year-old girl."

"Are you getting along with Ada?" my father asks. "You're not cooking up another divorce for us, are you?"

"We're managing. We work too hard. Work isn't good for lovers."

"I don't want to hear another word about it," my mother says, lowering her face into her hands. She could have been an actress. "You're unbelievable. Fabrizio, you know, I would be ashamed if I were you."

Crestfallen, my heart pounding, I venture: "Ashamed of what?"

"All the women you've known. Who do you think you are, Elizabeth Taylor?"

"It's not my fault if things fall apart. I'm not the only one involved, you know."

"Women today don't put up with men like your father."

My father glares at my mother. "What do you mean by that little remark?"

"Women need to be listened to."

"Oh, I see. So I didn't listen to you. You want a divorce, I guess."

"No, no, you listen to me. Like a mule."

"You see, Fabi? Who starts it, me or her?"

I can tell that things are heating up; I want to change the subject.

"Ada and I are all right. We're going to stay together. And there's Rasa. I won't abandon her."

"That's all we ask," my mother says, quickly, to avoid having an emotional outburst spin out of control.

My father pours me some wine and excuses himself from the table. He goes into the bedroom and comes back with his accordion. He sits at the table and begins to improvise. A waltz.

My mother claps her hands to the tune, which she recognizes. "It was when we were dancing to this waltz that your father and I first met. It was during the war of 1939. We were just kids. Imagine. Cupid shot an arrow through our hearts, and here we are, two old folks twisting with pain."

I clear the table, moving to the rhythm of the waltz that floated up from under my father's fingers, accompanied by little comments from my mother. I wash the dishes. The wine has softened my mind. I have the feeling a nap would do me a world of good. I have a headache.

"I love your music, Papa, but I think I'd better lie down. If I don't, I might fall down instead. My plane is at midnight, and I don't think I'll last. I love you, dear parents."

"Go, go," my father tells me. "Don't trouble yourself over us. Make yourself at home. No compliments. Go on, go to bed."

I give my mother a kiss on the forehead and go to lie down on the chesterfield in the living room. The blinds are closed. The room is dark. It's like a bedroom in a summer home in Termoli. I fall asleep to the rhythm of the waltz, like a baby in his mother's belly.

22

Marise is standing in the entrance of the Dai Baffoni restaurant, a cane in her hand. I go over to her and put my arms around her.

I help her sit down in front of me. She seems so tired, so terribly tired. I notice the red spots her age has painted on her face and hands, yet Marise is as ravishing a beauty at forty-eight as she was at fourteen.

I have the impression I wouldn't have succeeded in giving her the happiness other men have given her. It wouldn't have been within my powers. I can't imagine her putting up with a nervous man like me for years and years.

I don't have the courage to admit this to her. It's true – you can love people without being able to live with them.

I turn around in circles, I murmur some stupid bits of small talk.

Confiding in her that she was the woman I have most loved, in all my life . . . well, that's another matter.

When I say that at fourteen I was bitterly jealous of the boys that surrounded her, and that it was precisely this jealousy that led to our breakup, Marise doesn't know what I'm talking about.

She remembers me as always being kind and attentive to her needs.

"But we always had these fights about my jealousy! After I put an end to our relationship, I started going to a psychiatrist so I could get rid of those reactions. They were like emotional handcuffs. My jealousy made me vulgar and brutal."

No, what she remembers is the time I got after her for having dirty feet.

"You told me I needed to wash my feet more often."

"How could I have said a ridiculous thing like that to such a beautiful girl? How uncouth! The worst of it is, I remember very well how it happened. It wasn't a criticism. At the time, I hadn't learned how to bring off an elegant side-swipe; I just went at things head on. Since then, I've learned to be more tactful, to hide my reproaches under charm and seduction. I used to be too blunt. In some ways, I still am. What can I say? Feet turn me on. Make me fall head over heels."

She laughs at the pun.

"You can take the boy out of the country, but you can't take the country out of the boy. Urban civility is an acquired taste. It's a habit you develop slowly. Sometimes it takes decades."

Marise knows what I'm talking about. She prefers not to hear it, and especially not from me.

I should be more careful. I need to learn to think before I talk. I blurt out every idiotic thought that crosses my mind.

It isn't what you say that you need to say, but what you don't say. You have to say what's in your heart, and not what's on your mind. You have to say what you ought to say, because time is of the essence, and because, in the end, if you don't say it, you never will. And the other person will never know anything about it. The other will never know what you really think.

I don't believe and yet I do, I do really believe that a man could leave a mature woman like Marise for one who is younger, more shapely, prettier, better endowed in her erogenous zones. It's possible, reasonable, that someone could leave his wife when she's in her forties and leave his children for some bunny whose estrogen is running wild. That's not the hard part. I would even venture to say it's natural.

What is not so easy to understand is the idea that a man like me would be prepared to give everything up for this woman who is no longer young, with three children, who needs a cane to walk, this lawyer who is so-so about her work, who has a mind narrower than that of my younger wife. What desire, what ardour would push such a man over the cliff into the adventure of this kind of sentimental journey?

I don't know anything about human beings. I don't understand myself at all. Every time someone pokes a finger into some wrinkle of my personality, the fabric of it pulls tighter and the wrinkle disappears. I'm like a piece of fabric, shrunken, with an infinite number of threads to pull on. I hide in the folds and wrinkles that are flattened out under the touch of the fingers of those I love.

I don't know why it is that I always want what I can't have.

She tells me that her knees have gotten really bad; her backaches are terrible; she suffers from ulcerative colitis.

Her cane is made of black plastic; two screws hold the two parts together and can be pulled out or pushed in to make the cane longer or shorter. The curved handle handsomely slips into the palm of her delicate hand.

I'm trying to find an ideal adjective to describe Marise's hands. I can't. I have a weakness for her hands. They are slender, with aristocratic, flat, straight nails. Trimmed neatly. She wears a wedding band on her right ring finger. This surprises me a bit, because she's been separated for nearly a year.

"It's the only jewellery I have that's worth anything."

I touch her right hand. She averts her gaze.

"What a pleasure it is for me to be here, looking at you. I must say . . ."

I hold back, although I want to rush forward, headlong. I advance when I want to control myself, I laugh, I try to break the iceberg that's been there, between us, for as long as we've known each other.

She says she loves me the way you might love a tree.

"I'm happy that you love me the way you love a tree," I tell her.

I tell her about my last trip to New York.

She confesses she's never been there.

I'm ready to call my travel agent. Right now.

"Let's go together. Tonight."

She smiles, doubtfully.

I know I'm not kidding.

She asks me how my love life is going.

"I think about being happy."

"I don't know what happiness is. I don't know what love means. I only know one thing, and that's that I have to pay attention to my own little life."

We talk about politics, about the way the country is swinging to the right, about the discouragement in the new left wing.

"In a world where small businesses are bought up by large companies that are bought up by larger corporations, the morality of the left no longer has any clout."

"I am going to stay faithful to the left. I reinforce my determination by reading and thinking. I don't know what to think about the religious quests of people of our generation, though."

She asks me how long I've been a vegetarian.

I tell her it has been about ten years. In fact, my diet hasn't really changed; I still love to eat well, to drink, to smoke a cigarette once in a while.

"You talk about being a vegetarian as if it were a handicap."

She eats her veal, and I return to my pasta.

We drink a bottle of red wine; I can't remember what kind.

I have a good memory for things that happened a long time ago, but my memory falls apart when I try to recall what I did yesterday. As soon as it happens, it's gone. I admire people who remember the colour of the clothes they wore for some important occasion. Or the kind of shoes they were wearing or what they ate.

Half of my existence has escaped my recall. I try to reconstruct little islands of facts and bridge them together.

"There are certain events worth remembering. Others I file away in a drawer in my mental filing cabinet. But I forget the folder's there as soon as the drawer is shut. The files I believed were so essential to my survival are emptying out. It's the moments that seemed unimportant that endure."

She concludes that my life is composed of great gaps and blank spaces, covered in snow and cold. "It's the sun of my presence that your life lacks," she says, laughing.

I talk about the phone calls we used to make when we were young. In thirty-three years, the telephone rang pretty often.

"You call for help when you need a connection between what you're experiencing and what you're going to experience. I'm a link in a long chain between your past and your future. I'm lucky enough to be of some use to you. But you refuse to have any real love connection with me. You didn't choose me yesterday, and you won't choose me tomorrow."

"That's right. As soon as the link is repaired, I put you out the door, and you find yourself alone, with no woman in your life. You're a fool. I love you, and I need to share my secrets with you, not with anyone else."

"I'm a friend. But friendship isn't love. I want to take you into my arms and make you roar. I don't want to just be a friend. I don't want to be your buddy, I want to have a special place in your heart. I want to be your lover. I want you to think about me all the time. Obsessively."

She says that friendship is more durable than love, and I, myself, prefer to burn myself out like a match between her fingers rather than to find myself in the trash heap of friendship.

We are, in the end, strangers to each other.

"I'm the man for you, the love of your life. I'm convinced. I want to be with you, like air in the lungs of a drowning woman."

"This time, if you separate, it won't be my fault. You're not available. You're married to Ada, and you're crazy about her."

"Does being a husband shorten my shot at being a lover? Does marriage defeat passion?"

I feel desperately lonely, violently pulled away from my desire. Rising up inside of me is a rage that is capable of doing great harm. I'm disgusted with myself. I hate myself for not being able to give myself completely to Marise.

I don't want to get violent. I abhor violence. I want to force myself, out of love, through my silent, attentive presence, to disappear into her, like the wine she is drinking, caressing her cheeks from inside, going down her esophagus, I want to lapse into a state of reverie. I keep my distance, without touching her, as far away as possible from her daily life, and yet I want to be as simple and necessary to her as a glass of water.

I don't dare touch her. I'm afraid of offending her; I'm afraid of hurting her.

It's so difficult to love. It's so difficult to be loved.

We are outside.

It's late, later than I thought. I'll never make my plane to Dorval.

There's traffic on Saint-Laurent, lots of traffic. The weekend is beginning. People want to get away from their work, live out their fantasies that rise up in the air like the noise of cars plunging forward in the lit-up night.

I take Marise's arm and show her out to the car. She stops and says, "I want to touch you, to take your feet in my hands and rub them; I want to make love with you."

"I don't want to leave Ada. It's important for my daughter."

"Let's be grown up. Use me to forget your past."

"But you're part of my past."

"Not anymore."

23

My daughter won't stop talking. She's refusing to go to Junior Kindergarten. She wants to stay with me, sitting at her table, which she has pushed next to mine. She wants to talk to her imaginary playmates, with me, who is no less real than her friends sitting around her in my office.

She insists that I not watch her. I have to work. At least, I have to pretend to work, and I certainly can't stare at her.

I don't look at her.

She's working. She's playing at working. She's playing.

She asks me how you put staples in a stapler.

Her question is more than a question. It's an order, requiring my immediate attention.

"Papa, I want to talk to you. I want you to talk to me. I want us to spend more time together."

I stop what I'm doing and kneel down beside her. I listen to her. The telephone rings, the fax hums, and I don't move from the floor. I become her big brother. I'm not in the least interested in being her servant, but I am, whether I like it or not. I disappear from myself.

I become her horse, wild and strapping, obeying her orders when she commands me to get down on my hands and knees. Rasa loves horses, especially real ones, because she can no longer get up on the other, plastic kind.

One day, the mother of her friend Aube went to the zoo and took Rasa. Usually, I hate this lending and borrowing of children, but with Aube's mother, every obstacle I could put up vanished.

Suzanne is an Acadian from New Brunswick. No one can refuse her anything. As soon as she first spoke to me in French, all of my armour lifted from my body and flew away. It was the first time in five years I was alone in the house.

I may be Italian, but something vibrates inside me whenever I hear French. It's because of the connection I make between this manner of speaking and the dialect I use with my parents ever since I was a child.

So that Saturday, Rasa rode on a real pony. In the evening, when we knew she had drifted off into her dreams, Ada and I said to each other: "That's it. Now she's going to ask us to buy her a pony."

Oddly enough, it didn't happen. Her enthusiasm for horse-back riding is much deeper than that. Deeper than the words she possessed to try to explain her experience. She has decided she is going to be a veterinarian when she grows up.

Ada and I expect this childhood wish to come true.

Marise tells me that her sex, since the birth of her twins, is not what it used to be.

I tell her she's crazy.

"There is nothing more marvellous than the sex of a woman who has given birth to a child."

She looks at me, enraptured. No one has ever spoken to her like this before. It's an intimacy that her own husband refused to share with her.

"I can prove it to you, right here, in the van."

It's true. I'm ready to get down on my knees and gamble away my entire life, Ada, Rasa, my material possessions, my very existence, to show her just how wrong she is to think she's ugly.

At forty-eight years of age, she is a breath of fresh air that crosses this calm and clean construction that has become my daily routine since I've been living in Toronto.

Trisa keeps repeating in her emails to me that I left Montreal like a teenager who runs away from home. Trisa is right. The reason I packed my bags and ran off remains a mystery.

One day or another, everyone has to say goodbye to his parents and deal with real life. It's too easy to stay in your room, like a spoiled child who clings to his mother's bosom. Like it or not, the alarm rings and the lights on the highway alert us to the fact that the time has come to go.

I don't know why, but Marise is the one I choose to pull me out of my complacency. It's as though my Toronto home replaced my peaceful, soft-slippered Montreal life that I left behind nearly ten years ago.

Everything in the residence is in order, and then a woman knocks at the door. You go to open it because you're ready to open up to someone else. The stranger comes in and makes herself at home, among the cobwebs, in the entryway that leads right into your heart. You feel as though you've let this space get run down. Yes, you can recognize the little, narrow room with the window overlooking the park next door, full of sugar maples and chestnut trees. Why does this room seem to be of secondary importance? Every alcove matters. Every nook and corner, every hallway offers some shelter.

You can't pretend, make do. I tried that. No angle is less important than another one. Getting old means understanding that the big picture, however vast or minuscule, is actually all made up of small pieces.

I believed I could escape the presence of other women.

As for my human relationships, I'm going through a tragic period. Socializing isn't easy. It's impossible to seduce or be seduced.

Medicine and the Church have led us to act as though we're paranoid. Complicity between a man and a woman, even if it has been drastically compromised, altered almost beyond recognition, still seems possible.

Rejection. You have to learn to live with it, get through it. You're cast aside.

Ada rejects me often. She declines any offer to make love, any caress, any innuendo, any advance. But she insists she loves me. Her words don't erase my doubts. I don't believe her, she doesn't love me, she loves Rasa and that love is enough for her.

Scientists waste millions of American dollars every year looking for solutions for men's biological "handicap." At the end of the day, females will always be the ones who carry in their wombs the past and the future of humanity. The mate is replaceable, disposable. The man is unimportant, a cherished plaything.

In this sense, Robin Baker is right: biology continues to play an important role in the evolution of the relationship between men and women. The media exhausts itself trying to make us believe that young maidens are synonymous with beauty and longevity. Indeed, they bear the promise of long life – not for the male, but for the newborn.

We're all bad fathers or bad mothers. That's part of the job description. You have to be somewhat innocent to have children and blissfully unaware in order to raise them. That's why I think it's better to have them young, when everyone and everything is beautiful and sweet. As you get older, you become a mirror, and it's harder to hold the mirror up to your child.

I say to Marise, "You've become more resilient because of your children. This strength simply adds to the beauty of your body. You're not a procreative machine, but a being who is at last free."

She takes my hand and says nothing. Silence is often the best way to accept a crazy idea.

I tell myself, if I have to be unfaithful, I have to do it with dignity. The promise of fidelity lingers on. It's important to be able to give and receive the love that belongs to an aging body.

Young passion is careless. Young people give the way they receive, without worry, without awkwardness. If there is sincerity, the wave rolls out, its force is unleashed faster than apologies and forgiveness.

Pride is an uncomfortable burden. The refusal to analyse circumstances and impulses that drive the body to express its millions of years of existence. The brain's fugue is relatively young. I didn't invent this idea. It's brilliant: the body is older than the brain.

Muscles think more quickly than our grey matter. The wisdom a person acquires while aging comes from the fact that the head finally manages to understand the complexity of the body which, for its part, stays plugged into the survival circuit.

Coming dangerously close to Marise signifies that my psychic aging has acquired the knowledge held by my muscles.

Far be it from me to impose myself on Marise. There are no other barriers to remove. What is holding me back is the hand that emerges from inside myself. Am I going against and around my destiny?

My history is reaching its conclusion. I enter, proudly, the world that I'm creating. Marise enters, proudly, the world she is creating.

I don't know what comes over me. Refusing her invitation would be like killing myself. What is more painful: to cry or to laugh?

I imagine myself naked, and time becomes space and space becomes a wave of light that penetrates our bodies. Wonder. I tell her that I would like to be able to caress her sex with my tongue. I don't have the courage to follow through on my wish. I don't know what urge drives me to admit to this fantasy.

"We have twenty years to catch up on," she says.

I assure her that my patience is proof that we are on the same wavelength. She lights a cigarette that she consumes like a gulp of wine. She says that smoking, under these circumstances, is an escape. I smoke three cigarettes a day.

"I want you to put your tongue between my thighs," she says, looking out the open window of the van.

"Here?"

I feel a ball of flames travel from my heart to my belly. I don't know if I'm getting excited or getting an ulcer.

I hold her hand to get myself under control, so I won't explode like a frog swollen with water.

Marise has had too much to drink. I offer to drive her home.

She gets out of the van and I take my seat behind the wheel and, somehow, I don't know how, shift into reverse. The van rolls back.

Marise drops her cane and miraculously avoids the rear bumper of the vehicle. I put on the brake, but it is too late. Marise's cane is crushed under the rear wheel, on the passenger side. I get out, I try to apologize, Marise is beside herself.

"You could have killed me."

My eyes come up against the gaze of a murderous eagle.

"I'm an idiot."

"An absolute idiot."

I want to comfort her.

Marise squawks, pushing me with all her strength.

Now why in the world would my unconscious have played such a stupid trick on me? I'm opposed to physical violence. I'm confronted with the weakness that would have encouraged me to eliminate the woman who put me in such a state of bewilderment.

Marise deserves much more respect.

The possibility of loving two people at the same time presents itself to me as a futile exercise, completely unfeasible, an emotional acrobatic pose that I couldn't hold for any length of time.

Lea Simon was the one who taught me a few things about that. What a relief it was when she announced that she was going to move to Israel with Mario Berger. I got the full benefit – that was a strangely accurate word to describe our deal – from their decision to back *Antigone Pacifica*, which allowed me to finish it.

Her departure released me once and for all from the burden of a perilous passion. Going back to that kind of thing would have killed me.

I'm not brilliant. I go two steps forward and one step back as I try to make out the meaning of the indistinct future before me. I can no longer read the messages written on our skin the way I used to. I have to make it all up as I go along, figure out new lyrics to fit the rhythm of my reason, with all its burps and bumbles, as it struggles through its confusing movements.

It's through reason that we discover love. Dante says something like that in *La Divina Commedia*. And yet his emotions tie him to Beatrice. It's easy to shout out, "Reason, help me!" when reason has fled.

The heart is there for something: it is there to repair the damage when the intellect throws garbage in every direction.

Where can I run when emotion tears off the clothes I'm wearing? I'm standing in front of this stranger, the person I dare call my first love. I can't decide if I should drag her onto the futon or rush towards the exit.

The worst of it is that reason has no exit. Only by flattening reason through unbridled imagination can I save myself.

I act as though my brain was popped like a balloon by Cupid's arrow.

I prefer Ovid the Vegetarian to Dante the Catholic.

Apollo's first love is Daphne. Proud of his victory over the colossal serpent Python, Apollo uses a condescending tone when he talks to Cupid, who is wiping the string of his bow: "Little one, what are you doing with such a weapon? You want to play hard ball. I'm a tough guy. I can conquer wild animals."

The child isn't afraid. He answers: "Apollo, with your bow, you can pierce anything. With mine, I can pierce you. Animals are under your power, but you are under mine."

Cupid beats the air with his wings and goes to sit in the shade of a tree on Mount Parnassus. He shoots two arrows that have opposite effects. One creates love; the other destroys it.

He wounds Apollo with the first arrow. He immediately falls in love with Daphne, whom Cupid strikes with the second arrow.

The nymph escapes into the woods. Apollo runs after her.

Daphne has many suitors, but she ignores all of them. A winged and solitary Daphne wanders through the woods until she can no longer move.

The wind carries off her clothes.

Apollo follows her, step by step, like a dog in pursuit of a hare.

Pale, breathless, Daphne falls to her knees and begs heaven to come to her aid.

Apollo stops in front of the goddess and notices that a thin bark has begun to grow on Daphne's breasts.

He presses his lips to her, and she is slowly transformed into a tree. The tree bark repulses Apollo's kiss.

"Because you won't be my wife, you will be my tree."

He falls in love with the tree.

So every summer Apollo adorns his head with a branch of flowering laurels.

The sun drips its warmth down the trunk of the tree.

A river nestles calmly under the blue sky. The laurel tree bends its branches and shakes its upper leaves like a head.

I say, "It's like I've been chasing after you my whole life. I followed you around aimlessly, never knowing whether I should jump into a new affair or retreat into the forest of my obsession."

The older I get, the less I know about love.

I'm more ignorant at forty-eight than I was at eighteen.

Still, I'm curious. I'm curious about what Marise's body would feel like under my fingertips.

Lovers are in crisis because no one knows what makes them lovers, what keeps them together as a couple.

We're in her bed. Naked. The magic smoke from the hashish has lost its effect.

We look at each other, quietly.

"Desire disappears if it isn't nurtured," says Marise.

I wonder how I can reply to the comment. I don't say anything at all. I ease closer to her.

We stay there, without budging, in the quasi-dusk of her big, almost empty room. There isn't much furniture: a turn-of-the-century dresser and chair. A modernist painting with a red sphere in a square. It's the work of an important painter I don't know.

Marise takes me by the arm, pulls my whole body over hers. Her eyes are wide open. I place my lips awkwardly on her forehead.

"Make love to me," she tells me. "I'm not looking for anything lyrical. That would be amazing. I don't know what I'm looking for in you. What do people look for in each other? Themselves? Something different? Maybe I'm looking for my opposite."

"I want to talk about you, because I want to, and for me that's enough. Guilty or not. Insist without insisting. Presence wins every time."

"I don't like humiliating or being humiliated. If you think I'm clinging, say so. I have nothing to lose. You have to be able to declare your love. I don't want to offend you or hurt you."

I move closer to Marise's face. I want to see her smile, but can't. I take her face between the palms of my hands and place my lips on hers. I kiss her, a long kiss, without opening my mouth. I want it to be my lips that speak of a love that is still alive for her.

No.

I get up out of bed. I ask her to call me a taxi. I want to leave. I tell her I will always be there to help her, that if she ever needs me she just has to call. But, in the middle of this grand moment of tenderness, I need to go. I can't continue. I don't know why.

Marise says nothing. Or so little. A few insignificant words.

She stretches out towards the telephone on the night table, where there is a pile of romance novels, and says, "You have learned to surrender to love and to passion without becoming their slave."

24

I arrive on 19th Avenue, at my sister's house. Lucia bought our parents' house.

Police cars line the street. I have to get out of the taxi and walk the rest of the way.

The door is ajar. Lucia is planted behind it. It's me she's waiting for. She dissolves into tears as soon as she catches sight of me.

"It's Peter!"

I don't understand. She points towards the policemen.

"Peter?"

"Yes. He's here."

I ask her where he is.

She doesn't answer. She stares at the cars and I turn around to look more closely at the policemen. There are plainclothes cops with guns in their hands.

"Peter is sitting in the car," she says.

I can make out the silhouette of a man on the back seat of one of the police cars.

"Where are they taking him?" I ask her in our dialect.

"He's a madman, I'm telling you. A sick, sick man."

She explains how the police officer announced that Peter had committed at least ten hold-ups in a row around Toronto. He is a hashish dealer for the mafia in Saint-Michel.

Do I have the courage to tell her that I had the honour of attending one of the hold-ups that very morning?

I have no choice.

I tell her everything I know about her husband.

"You have no idea what I've been going through for the past sixteen years," Lucia says.

"You have to leave him."

"Impossible."

I fix my eye on the police cars more clearly. The officers are preparing to leave. I take Lucia by the arm and close the door. The little girl is in bed, sleeping.

"No, I'm not calling Papa!"

It's useless to insist. Lucia is stubborn. Once she gets an idea in her head, there's nothing anyone can do about it.

I ask her if I should stay the night. She says no.

I don't want to leave her alone with her problems. She must be suffering. She is probably ashamed. She's at the centre of such commotion. All the neighbours, behind their curtains, have a bit of an idea of what's happening. Her secret is out.

Ten o'clock at night.

I have to decide whether to stay or go. My plane won't wait. I sit down on a chair in the kitchen of our childhood, the same kitchen where she first introduced us to Peter Hébert.

The kitchen hasn't changed. Lucia doesn't have the courage it would take to decorate it the way she'd like.

"The walls have too many memories," she says, sipping a glass of water.

I get up and stroke her hair. No word of consolation comes out of my mouth. We sit down and count the veins in the grain of the wooden kitchen table.

"Are you sure you don't want me to spend the night here? I can take a morning flight instead."

She talks softly, confessing that she'd rather be alone. She can take the little one over to our parents' place.

"How is Eve?" I ask.

Eve is fine. Eve is no longer a child. Eve is sixteen. Eve has a boyfriend. Eve will be starting Cégep soon. Eve is taking driving lessons.

Lucia is impatient. She tells me she's going to call a lawyer. She needs to get her husband out of jail.

I tell her she'd be better off forgetting that and give herself time to catch her breath.

Lucia gets angry and makes it clear that I have no right to meddle in her affairs.

No one should stick his nose into the space between a husband and a wife.

When I ask her if she knew about her husband's illegal goings-on, Lucia doesn't answer.

"You don't think I'm just going to toss him into the garbage can, do you? Peter Hébert is my child's father."

I have an urge to tell her a stupid joke about the difference between men and women, but I stop myself, even though a little humour might lighten the mood. Lucia loves to laugh. It would do her good.

"Do you have a newspaper handy?"

"A newspaper?"

"I want to read my horoscope."

She hands me a copy of the *Journal de Montréal* from the pile of old newspapers she keeps next to the fridge.

She flips through the pages, licking and clicking her fingers, until she gets to the horoscopes. She reads: "You can't avoid your exes. Thanks to them, you will learn many things, among them the importance of not chewing over the errors of your past."

"Strange, because today I ran into Thomas and Marise."

"Were they together?"

"No, I saw them separately. Thomas asked me for some sperm to make a baby, and Marise . . ."

"You slept with her."

"Almost."

Lucia laughs: "You couldn't get it up."

"Something like that."

I tell her to call a cab. I fold up the newspaper that Lucia has pushed to one side to throw into the recycling bin.

Lucia gives me a hug.

There's a tear in the corner of her eye. She closes the door and turns off the light on the verandah.

It's raining. The night air is cool.

I hold the newspaper over my head like an umbrella. One of Chopin's *Nocturnes*, performed by Stefan Askenase, plays in my head as I stand there.

25

"Here's my cue. This is where I come in."

It's the middle of the night. Someone is saying these words. I open one eye. With great effort, I manage to find Ada's hand under the covers. She's sleeping. It wasn't Ada who said it.

I roll out of bed and stumble into the kitchen. The blinds are up, the way I left them before I went to bed. I like to feel the morning sun burning into the house.

The neighbours are sleeping, all except one. The light of his TV is flickering, jumping up onto the walls of the dark room.

Still studying the windows, I drink some spring water directly from the spout of the bottle. Ada doesn't like it when I do that.

I feel good. There's no confusion in my head at all. I'm fully awake now.

The man from the hills – he has come to shake me.

I recognize the soft, reassuring voice.

Images spin, dance out of reach inside me.

I see him standing at my side, with simple clothes made of hemp. I burst out laughing, because I don't believe in angels. I don't believe in ghosts.

There was a time when I believed in the spirit world. Those days are over.

I want to live my life like a rat in a cage. I want to be free to turn around in circles, going over and over the same track in the maze I'm building in my head, through all the what if's and if only's. My life is a fiasco, and the lack of success keeps me from taking myself too seriously.

Failure has inflicted on me an acute consciousness of my role as a romantic doomed to play out the bad script my life has become. I'm tired of playing the idiot in the film. It doesn't even matter whether it's a good film or a bad one; I've had enough.

My thoughts are predicated on my beliefs that put a brake on any possibility of flying off in other directions.

No, the voice I hear is not issued by a soldier of the heavens, it's the voice inside me that is raised from the lining of my body, from my muscles. It's my blood's beat.

The vivacity of each syllable is reassuring.

The man who is talking, the thing in me that has shown up speaking like this, wants me to see it directly with no notion of good or evil.

I cross a wide field in a beige cotton robe. Beyond the hill, the sea murmurs. I walk up the side of the hill.

On the horizon stand the walls of a medieval city. I recognize this place. I lived there for a year.

The blue of the sky is glorious with the presence of human beings. No god is lurking, lying in wait behind the clouds. I know this geography well. I would even say that it's my home, despite the fact that international laws prevent me from naming a foreign land as my domicile.

I have the clear sense that I'm in familiar territory.

Contentment.

Here's my cue.

Here.

It's late. I'm tired. I can't sleep.

He knocks at my door. He comes and pulls off the covers, and leads me into these landscapes of the Middle Ages.

I walk up the hill towards the walls of the city and notice that the sandals I'm wearing don't come from Thomas's store.

I contemplate the ocean's calm.

Everything that is happening and that is surrounding me is familiar.

I'm not alone.

I try to catch the eye of the man from the hills who is walking at my side.

The man smiles at me. I smile back at him.

Together, we go up to the olive field.

He says in Italian, "*Sono Adamo*. I am Adam."

"I recognize your face. I don't know where I've seen you before."

Adamo continues walking, his eyes going from the sky to the sea, moving calmly and intensely.

I notice that he doesn't squint in the bright daylight.

Adamo catches me staring at him. He says, "You know where you are. You are where you are supposed to be."

It's the Adriatic.

Adamo nods his head.

I stop, placing my hand on his hand in a gentlemanly gesture.

What am I doing here? I should be in bed, asleep.

"Don't you think you've slept long enough?"

Adamo drinks in the sea.

"For more than a century you've been carrying the world on your shoulders. You must be sick of it."

I lower my eyes. I put my hands over my face. A century rolls by me.

"It was easier, sleeping in weeds and poison sumac . . ."

. . . . than balancing on the axis of the earth.

I take my hands from my face. I'm alone.

Adamo is way ahead of me already, standing before the gates of the city.

I run, trying to catch up to him. I have so many questions to ask him.

It's too hot. Sweat is a burden that gets in the way. I sit down, forcing myself to catch my breath.

The sun rusts the earth.

I call Adamo.

He's no longer there.

I haul myself up from the burning sand. I cross through the gates and lose myself in the devoted and radiant crowd.

I look all over the place, but I can't find Adamo.

I take off into the lane. My short sprint becomes a meandering stroll.

I wander through the labyrinth of the city.

I hear the echo of my footsteps on the flagstones of volcanic rock.